TATE McCOY SERIES ☼ BOOK 1

MY SO-CALLED RUINED LIFE

BY MELANIE BISHOP

TORREY HOUSE PRESS, LLC

SALT LAKE CITY · TORREY

First Torrey House Press Edition, January 2014
Copyright © 2014 by Melanie Bishop

Published by Torrey House Press, LLC
P.O. Box 750196
Torrey, Utah 84775 U.S.A.
www.torreyhouse.com

International Standard Book Number: 978-1-937226-21-3
Library of Congress Control Number: 2013952249

Cover art by Christy Hawkins • christy-hawkins.com
Cover and book design by Jeff Fuller, Shelfish • Shelfish.weebly.com

This book is dedicated to all the young people in my life: nieces, nephews, great-nieces and great-nephews, Godkids, and all my students, current and former.

MY SO-CALLED RUINED LIFE

CHAPTER ONE:

RUIN

It's one thing to lose your mom shortly before your sixteenth birthday. It's another thing to know she was murdered. When they decide it's your dad who did the murdering, nobody cares that you disagree. He is hauled off; you are farmed out. If you are wondering about now how this could get any worse, try living with this fact: you and your mother had not been getting along—barely speaking—for almost two years.

Saying it in second person doesn't make it better. This didn't happen to *you*, it happened to me. But some hypothetical *you* can use the terms "mother" and "mom," which aren't words that have come out of *my* mouth for some time. Since we'd stopped speaking, I'd referred to her as Carla. Like some distant relative, a second cousin twice removed, maybe someone I'd never even met. Therefore, someone I couldn't possibly miss.

While I know there's no way *my* dad did it, apparently dads far and wide are capable of this. If you watch TV shows like *Dateline* or *48 Hours*, you know how common it is for people to kill their spouses. Mostly it's men who kill their wives, but it happens the other way too. In fact, the minute someone is murdered, they will look first of all at the spouse. Some don't even pretend to be grief-stricken. A man on the show calls up 911, says my wife's dead on the floor, and doesn't shed a tear.

I don't watch these shows because they're good. They are, in fact, some of the worst journalism you can find. I watch because my father is on trial for the murder of his ex-wife, Carla, and there are reporters in the courtroom. These so-called reporters from *48 Hours* and *20/20* and *Dateline* have tried to talk to me. I watch to prepare myself for when my own family's tragedy shows up as entertainment on prime-time TV.

The shows are terrible—even if the topic is riveting. They repeat everything a minimum of five times (I've counted), and after each commercial break they review the tale from the beginning, in case someone has decided to tune in mid-show. They flash the same pictures on the screen, over and over—the woman, beautiful and happy, smiling with her children. Family portraits where you'd never dream someone was thinking of killing someone else in the photo. And then there are the graphic crime scene pictures—blood-soaked carpets and mattresses, a body on the laundry room floor. They interview friends of the deceased who usually say something like, *The minute I heard she'd been killed, I knew it was him.* Sometimes, if the producers of the show are lucky, the friend is able to provide a letter in which the woman wrote those very words: *If ever I turn up dead, he's the one who did it! I fear for my life every day.* That sort of thing.

Lots of the people who commit these crimes do so because they have fallen in love with someone else and think the only way out of one marriage and into another is to kill the spouse who stands in the way of the new, improved model. Again, this stuff seems obvious to me, but who would want to become the new wife of a man who just offed the first one? What's to stop him from later doing the same thing to you? And how is it that people get married to someone they're later going to want to kill? Why does a woman ever stay married to a man who makes her fear for her life? And why, as in many of these badly televised cases, does the husband think the only way out of a marriage is to murder the wife? Hello? People! Ever heard of divorce?

My parents had been divorced for two years and separated for four. My dad had no other lover, not that she would've cared if he did. She'd fooled around for their whole marriage, and, to use Dad's saying, would not have had a leg to stand on. She's the one who wanted the divorce in the first place, and their split was what they call "amicable." So it doesn't add up. Everyone you talk to in this town is pretty much of the mind that they rushed to accuse my dad, because when there are gory-ass murders of gorgeous women, people want someone behind bars—now.

I don't go to court every day like my dad's brothers do. At least one of them is there at all times—they do shifts. I've gone twice, and that was enough. Everyone thinks I don't go because it's a horrible thing for a kid to see and think about. But 1) I am not a kid. I'll be a junior next year. And 2) I'm not so delicate that I couldn't face it if I wanted to. And 3) Hard as it is for people to fathom, I am over the initial shock of all this—the murder was a year ago last month: June 12th. A year is a very long time. I don't go because I hate all the whispering about *the poor daughter*, and because I get tired of dodging those nosy reporters, but mostly because it seems like a waste of a summer, and I already lost last summer to this whole ordeal. I've got stuff I want to do. Besides, I think it's more helpful to my dad if I visit him, when we can have conversations, than it is to see him during the trial, when even smiling at the defendant from across the room is discouraged.

Among the many horrible things about this situation is all the therapy that gets forced on you, and I'm not even opposed to therapy in general—I think it's great and necessary and everyone should try it at least once. But enough can be enough. Pretty much everyone thinks I should be in therapy for the rest of my supposedly ruined life. I'm supposed to turn out a whack job. The relatives on both sides of the family are concerned: if I'm upset, they worry about me; if I'm not upset, they worry about me. There are only so many times you can rehash the story with a therapist, telling her how it all felt every step of the way. It starts to be as boring as *Dateline*.

Probably the worst of the aftershocks was when my boyfriend, Jasper Finch, broke up with me. His parents put me up for the first month after it all happened. The Finches are good people. But it freaked them out—I mean, who wouldn't be freaked out by a murder in their neighborhood? Everything that had been great between me and Jasper got overshadowed by it. Nobody wants to date a girl who has 1) mandatory therapy, 2) a mom in the grave, and 3) a dad in jail. I give people the heebie-jeebies. I'm a walking reminder of the whole mess. Ruin.

Here's a story about the kind of dad my dad is. When I graduated from 9th grade, the last year at the junior high, we were driving home from the ceremony and Dad said he had a surprise for me. (My mom had been at the ceremony, too, but we weren't getting along so I didn't say anything to her. I noted she was there, though.) I knew if there was a graduation present forthcoming, it would be from Dad, and sure enough, he started acting all sneaky on our way home. He wanted me to guess. He is very big on guessing games, and never considers that I might've outgrown them.

"A car," I said. This was a joke, because 1) I was not old enough to drive, and 2) we didn't have that kind of money.

"Right," he said. "Hot Wheels, how'd you know? Those little speedsters—and I got you the race track, too."

"Sweet," I said, going along with his joke.

"Guess again," he said.

"A mountain bike."

"Ah," he said. "We're doing the transportation category. Next you will guess boat or plane."

"Boat wouldn't be bad. One of those kayaks that you can take out on Lake Travis or Town Lake?"

"Well, Tate, I apologize, but it's not a boat. Nor an airplane. And not a choo-choo train, either."

"Just tell me already," I said.

"I want to see if you can guess. Come on, use your ESP."

He and I used to believe we had mental telepathy together. We could send each other telepathic messages. *What color am I thinking of? Which number between one and ten? Guess what we are having for dinner.* If I concentrated hard enough, and really envisioned my thoughts merging with his own brainwaves, I almost always got what he was thinking. He would brag about this to his colleagues.

"I'm rusty," I said. "How about giving me a hint?"

"It's something you want so badly you can't even think of it, because if you thought of it and voiced that guess and then it was *wrong*, you wouldn't be able to stand the disappointment." He looked at me then, for emphasis. The signal light we were stopped at went from red to green. "I'll go so far as to say..."

"Dad," I said, motioning with my chin toward the light. "Go."

The green light registered and he drove through the intersection before finishing his sentence.

"I would go so far as to say you probably think it's impossible that I would give you this particular gift at this particular time," he said.

There was only one thing he could've been talking about.

"You better not be lying," I said.

"I have never lied to you, you know that."

"Well, the only thing that I can think of that I have really, really wanted, like since I was thirteen, that you have always said was out of the question, is the guest house."

"Hmmm…" he said. And then, "Should we stop for some Thai take-out?"

"Dad! Don't change the subject!"

"I'm not," he said. "Rather, I am asking my daughter who just graduated from junior high *with honors*, if she would like to pick up a celebratory meal, the first that we will share in her new living space."

I let out a big scream. He told me to keep it down.

"You're not kidding?" I said. Suddenly everything out the car window was animated, more imbued with color, not the same drab view I'd seen every trip home from school for years.

"Tate, I would never be so cruel as to kid about something like this."

He told me he had planned it for a couple of months. That as soon as the recent tenant, a college student, had moved out after spring semester, he just wouldn't readvertise it. He always filled it with students he knew from the community college, where he was on faculty. He said it was a financial risk, not having a renter in there—but the finances were not for me to worry about. That was his responsibility. As long as I continued to be mature and responsible and keep the place tidy, he was happy to give me this new freedom and privacy. "You've earned it," he said.

When we got out of the car at Thai Castle, I assaulted him

with hugs. *Thank you thank you thank you, Dad.* He was right—I would've thought this was impossible, out of the question. Ever since the divorce, and paying for our house and Carla's house, and doing more work with his non-profit, which didn't pay as well, money was tight. He absolutely needed the rent from the guest house in our backyard in order to make the mortgage payments.

He assured me that he had a new source of income. Some consulting work on the side.

"Like I said, the finances of our household are mine to worry about," he said. "Now, see if you can guess what I'm going to order."

"Dad, that is not challenging in the least. You will have Pad Thai. You *always* have Pad Thai."

"Is that your official guess then?"

I nodded, as Dad held the door of Thai Castle open for me. He's big on the whole gentleman thing. Chivalry, he always reminds me, is not dead.

"Let me tell you what I think *you're* going to order," he said a little too loudly, like he was talking to a four-year-old. I let Dad know telepathically that we were in the restaurant now, and I was embarrassed to play the guessing game with people around. We were not the only family hitting this popular eatery, post-graduation.

"I'm embarrassing you?" he said. "Of course I am. We'll stop the shenanigans. We've got a public image to maintain."

And right then the woman showed up at the register to take our order, and Dad said, "My daughter will have the tofu with veggies." He looked at me for confirmation. I nodded. There are four things on this menu that I like, but he guessed it; tofu with veggies was what I was planning to order that night. Proud of his telepathic gift, he continued: "And I think I will have the Massaman curry, spicy." The waitress actually had to scratch Pad Thai off of the order tablet where she'd written it in advance. She and I looked at each other, like *Lo and behold, the creature of habit has ordered something new!*

"What?" he said. "A man can't change his mind? A man can't branch out and be adventurous? It's a new era," he said. And then, "We're celebrating Tate's graduation."

When we got home, he had the guest house ready. He'd set a nice table with my favorite tablecloth. It's blue, and has yellow chickens and white hens in a pattern all along the hemline. As a centerpiece, he had this cake holder pedestal thing, an antique from his own grandmother—mint green depression glass—and right in the center were two perfect replicas of eggs, one white and one yolk-colored, made out of Play-Doh. When I was little, he could make anything with Play-Doh and these so closely resembled real eggs, I only knew they were imposters by their distinctive Play-Doh smell.

"Oh my God!" I said, taking in a deep whiff. "Where did you even find Play-Doh?"

"They still make it," he said. "Compliments of Hasbro. Go ahead and choose one."

My dad is big on rituals. We used to play this game when I was little where he would take a small toy of mine—a roly-poly person from one of those Fisher Price farms, or one of my collection of dinosaurs, or a spike heel from Barbie's vacation wardrobe—and bury it in a ball of Play-Doh. And then he would make it into a shape, like a block or a sphere or a big triangle, or even something more difficult, like a bird or a banana. He'd make another one identically shaped, in a different color of clay. I had to guess (guessing is always part of Dad's games) if it was the red triangle or the blue one that held a toy inside. He was great at making the two shapes identical, one with hidden cargo, one without. I would use my telepathic powers to figure out which one held the toy. I used to think I really did have ESP, because I was right about half the time. But I know now how silly that was—the odds were always 50/50.

I went after the white egg, pretending to crack it on the table edge, just to humor Dad, then pulling it apart into two hunks, revealing the key to the studio, *my very own new house.* He had wrapped the key in cellophane so the Play-Doh wouldn't stick.

While we ate, he explained to me that he would always be moments away in the main house, and I should always feel free to sleep in my room there if I wanted to. I could go over and eat whatever he was having for dinner, or I could fix something in my own kitchenette. It's what every teenager dreams of—freedom, privacy, autonomy. A door that locks.

But the point of all this is, my dad, always afraid that Carla wouldn't do enough for me, doubled up on goodness. His main goal in life is to give me a really solid childhood, a really terrific start. This insanity that's going on now, so out of his control...well, it's killing him to think how it's affecting me.

I was only in the guest house for three weeks when our world fell apart.

After a month at the Finches, when Jasper broke up with me, I couldn't stay there anymore. They would have kept me, but it was sad and humiliating and I had already lost a lot. You cannot live with the family of your ex-boyfriend, hello. Once I convinced Dad and my Aunt Greta to let me move back into my guest house, they convinced the other relatives who'd taken up the business of hawking over me. So the deal is, for now anyway, someone from my mom or dad's family is in the main house at all times. They take turns. And I get my little studio in the back. This took a lot of convincing. Everyone is waiting for me to completely disintegrate. Delayed reaction to loss. Post-traumatic Stress Disorder.

I intend to make more of this summer than I made of the last one. I have goals up on a chart in the studio. I had them written in my notebook but my best friend Kale said *write them bigger and put them on the wall where they will stare at you every day.* So I did.

1. Learn to swim laps
2. Do some kind of volunteer work
3. Research colleges (and study for SATs)
4. Go camping with Aunt Greta
5. Find a part-time job (save money!)
6. No more boyfriends till I figure out my life (give it six months)
7. Be there for Dad (visit, bring favorite foods)
8. Redecorate studio (paint, get cool furniture)
9. Keep it neat (or else they will take it away!)
10. Become a vegan (and buy vegan cookbook)

Obviously Kale influenced #1 and #10. She's vegan and has been trying to get me to join her. And she's learned to swim laps for meditative reasons. She tells me there's nothing like the calm and the rhythm you reach after the first mile. You find your buoyancy, apparently, and it's heaven once you get the hang of it. If it works for Kale, I'm willing to try it. Kale named herself after her favorite leafy green. Up until tenth grade, Kale was Karen. She never liked that name.

My name's Tate—Tate McCoy—and I like it just fine.

CHAPTER TWO:

GOOSE BUMPS

Kale and I are stretching on the lawn at Barton Springs. It's 11a.m. and already a scorcher. Barton Springs is a long, natural limestone pool, spring-fed, and 68 degrees year-round. It's a thousand feet from one end of the pool to the other, three football fields long, where serious swimmers do their laps. Everyone out there now, some of them elderly, has swim caps on. They move through the water like human fish. They appear to not mind the cold.

"I can't believe I didn't think to get a one-piece," I say. I'm in the bathing suit I bought last summer, and it's a bikini.

"Next time," Kale says. She's arching her back and grabbing her toes in some yoga move.

I do a few lunges and sit-ups. Stretching has never been my thing.

"You really swim a mile here? That's impressive." I'm looking at the far end of the pool, wondering just how far it is.

"I'm telling you," says Kale, "learning to swim, the right way, will change the way you think about working out."

"I pretty much don't think about that at all."

"Well, that'll change, too. Once you get the hang of doing laps, you could go on forever. It's the most relaxing thing. And typically, people don't think of exercise as a form of relaxation."

"Excellent point, Leafy Green."

We go to the shallow section to get used to the temperature. Kale walks right in, dunks down, gets her head wet, and squeezes water from her hair. I'm having trouble going in past my ankles.

"It's freezing," I say.

"May I remind you this is Texas in July?" Kale says. "Freezing is a good thing." She disappears for a while, like an eel.

I get up to my thighs, but it's torture. All goose bumps.

A cute guy passes, trailed by a group of six kids—a lesson, obviously. I've seen him somewhere before, this guy.

Kale resurfaces next to me and squirts a fountain of water from her mouth into my face.

"Nice," I say. I splash her good. "Very mature. Plays well with others."

"So try a lap already!"

"Wait, check out that guy over there, the one teaching all the kids."

"Sawyer Madison," she announces. "He taught my lessons, too. He's good. I recommend taking a class, at least one. You learn a huge amount about how to breathe, how to relax, how to let yourself sink until you find your place of buoyancy, just below the surface."

"Where have I seen him before?"

"He goes to our school. Moved here last year."

I shake my head. "Wasn't at school. This is going to drive me crazy."

Kale is demonstrating buoyancy by floating on her back.

She says, "Did you know women with fake boobs float better?"

"You're not helping me figure out where I know this Sawyer guy from. I've totally seen him, like up close."

"Are we a wee bit obsessed?" says Kale.

"No. He's just familiar."

"Well, you should sign up for a lesson."

"Or a boob job, apparently," I say. "Okay, so teach me something. Anything."

Kale says, "Well, first you need to get all the way wet."

I suck in a breath and dunk myself.

"SHIT!"

"Now," says Kale, ignoring me, "swim with me over to that other side. Swim however you've been taught or however you're most comfortable."

I thrash about for ten strokes or so, unable to do the breathing thing without losing the rhythm and drinking the pool.

"Keep going," Kale says. "It should get easier. Let yourself get into a flow."

When I finally arrive at the other side, Kale is there waiting for me, watching.

"You beat me, of course," I say. I'm gasping. "Damn, there has to be an easier way. That just about killed me. I told you I'm not a natural in the water."

"The easiest way is to take a formal lesson. I could tell you what I think you're doing wrong, but I'd be guessing. Sawyer would be better. He even does a class for adults who are phobic, or can't stay afloat at all. You swim fine, you're just not graceful about it."

"Grace would definitely not be a word I'd use to describe what I just did."

I tell her I'm not about to make a fool of myself by swimming in front of Sawyer. "He's cute," I add.

Kale says, "Tate has a crush!"

"I don't! I've just seen him somewhere..."

Kale has had the same boyfriend since 9th grade—Simon—and they are a totally solid couple. She doesn't have to think about how she acts or how she looks. And maybe because of this, she acts great—always herself, never self-conscious, never trying to impress anyone. And she *looks* great, because, well, Leafy Green is gorgeous. She couldn't look bad if she wanted to.

I convince her to get in her mile of swimming without me. I'll practice. As she glides off she says, "Experiment with your buoyancy."

"Roger that," I say.

I watch her for a bit to see if I can learn by imitation. She looks perfectly synchronized—arms beating out a rhythm, feet gently propelling, head up on the left, now the right. When I try to do what she's doing, my whole body twists to get the breath. I need a more swivel-y neck. And then it happens. Every time I have any thought about my head or neck, I hear it. My brain conjures up the sound it must've made. Blunt object to her skull, not once, but sixteen times. The first one would've sounded very different from the last one. These thoughts take over. They torture me. I get out, get some money, and head to the concession for a lemonade. I drink it all at once, like it's medicine. And then I go back to our big old sheet spread out on the hillside, our four flip-flops holding down the corners. I plop down and close my eyes. If I can fall asleep, the sound of bludgeoning will go away. *Sixteen times.* One for each year I've been alive.

Next thing I know, swim teacher guy is standing over me.

"Tate," he's saying. I don't know how many times he's said it.

"Yes?" I prop up on one elbow, adjusting my bathing suit top.

"Kale said I should come talk to you?" He ends it in a question, like he's followed her orders, but he's uncertain what to say next.

"Oh did she? Leafy Green said that?"

"She said you have questions about lessons?"

"Not really. She was going to teach me to swim better, so I could do laps like she does, but our first lesson proved me to be a spaz of the highest order."

"But you can stay afloat?" he says. The sun blinds me when I look up at him.

"Sorry," he says. He moves to the left and his body blocks the sun.

"Yes, technically, I swim. I mean, I won't drown. But there's nothing fluid or efficient about it."

"Lessons would help," he says. "Everyone can learn what Kale learned. She wasn't that good either at first."

"She's good now," I say.

"She got the hang of it." Teacher boy looks uncomfortable. "I don't know how to say this…" he continues. "Can I sit down?"

"Sure." I sit up, to meet him halfway. I was horizontal, he was vertical; now we're both sitting on the sheet, face to face.

"I guess I'm just sorry for all you must be going through."

Here it comes. I nod. This is always awkward. I want to receive sympathy graciously, but I also don't want pity. I can't exactly say, "Oh, no biggie," because it's huge and everyone knows it.

"Thanks," is all I say.

"And I'm sure you feel confident about this already, but I think your dad's going to be acquitted."

"Oh, he's definitely innocent," I say.

"I agree," says Swimmer Boy. "Pretty much everyone thinks so, except the prosecution of course. But then that's their job."

"That's where I've seen you before! At the trial! It was driving me crazy—you looked so familiar."

"I can explain that," he says. "Journalism project."

I take in Sawyer Madison, with this new knowledge of him. "I only went to court twice," I say, "but you were there both times. You took notes."

"Right. The newspaper advisor at school thought it would be good practice for me, since I want to be an editor of a college paper. He suggested I attend the trial this summer and report on it. He thought it would be stupid not to, as a journalist living in this town when this thing happens. He thinks if I cover it well, I could even publish something."

"Cool."

"I guess I wanted to say…" Swimmer Boy looks to the left, looks to the right, looks anywhere but right at me.

"You're sorry," I say.

"I already said that," he says. He smiles. "I wanted to say I admire you."

No one has said this to me before.

"You seem to be handling this tragedy in your life very gracefully."

"Yeah, maybe that's why I swim so badly. All my grace is used up." (When in doubt, make a dumb joke.)

Sawyer lets out a little laugh.

"Really, though, what else can I do? There's not a thing I can do to change any of it."

"Well," he says, "I saw you a few weeks ago, in court, and I heard those women sitting behind you—I was in their row, and I heard what they said. I thought you handled that really well."

"Which comment was that?"

"They said you'd never have a normal life."

"Yeah. That's a warm and fuzzy comment for sure."

"And what's normal anyway?" says Swimmer Boy.

"Good point." I see Kale walking toward us, surveying her handiwork.

"Anyway, if you decide you want lessons, I'd like to do it no charge."

"Thanks. I'll keep that in mind."

"Keep what in mind?" says Kale. She's knocking her head on the side to get water out of her ears.

"Lessons," I say. "You sent Mr. Instructor my way."

"He has a name," says Kale. "Sawyer. And he's a good teacher." Kale lies down and puts a shirt over her face. "Wake me up before I get too burned."

"That's a cool name, by the way," I say. "After Tom Sawyer?"

"No. After my dad."

"He's Sawyer also?"

"No," says Swimmer Boy. "Carpenter. Sawyer equals one who saws."

"Seriously? I love that! Did you hear that, Kale? Kale and I are word freaks. That is just so *cool*." Okay, I tell myself, pipe down. Don't go overboard.

"Does having that name mean your parents want you to go into carpentry?"

Sawyer gets up.

"I want to be a reporter," he says. "They know that."

"Right."

He says, "Well, I've got another group coming in ten minutes. Let me know if you want free lessons."

"Would I be with a group of little kids like that?"

"No. There are adult groups, but we could do private."

The way he says the word makes me think of other things

I would like to do with this swimmer boy in private. I remind myself quickly of Goal #6.

"Thanks," I say. "Very generous of you, one-who-saws."

He smiles.

"See ya," he says. "Bye, Kale."

"Later," she says, without moving the T-shirt from over her face.

"Ta-ta," I say as he walks away. He shoots back a quick wave.

"You did *not* just say that." She comes out from under her sunshield.

"Oh my God," I say, and we burst into laughter. "He must think I'm such a dork!"

This is a private joke between me and Kale. We throw out as many funny versions as we can of greetings when we first see each other, and of goodbyes when we part ways. We don't generally do this in front of other people. The whole thing started when our third grade teacher—Mrs. O'Connor—taught us letter writing—business letters, personal letters, postcards. For some reason, we found the word *salutation* a riot. This is the part of the letter where you say Dear so and so, but in our text book, it gave alternatives, like *Greetings!* Or *Top of the mornin' to you!* That one cracked us up. We collected these like other kids collect scout badges or baseball cards. Ta-ta! Toodles! Regards to the family! All the best!

"That is so a sign, dude," Kale says, lying back down and going under cover.

"Sign of what?"

"Nothing."

"Tell me."

"Can't."

"Why not?"

"Violates one of the goals on your wall."

"Tell me or I will have to pummel you senseless."

Kale lifts the cover off her eyes for a sec, to give me a certain skeptical look she has.

"What?" I say.

"That last comment. It's sort of not funny, given events in your recent past."

"True," I say. "Ugh. Totally poor taste. Sorry." And for a minute I've got that kicked in the gut feeling again. Kale has seen me when I slide into this funk.

"You okay?" she says.

"Yes. But tell me, what is 'ta-ta' a sign of?"

"Just that you *accidentally* felt comfortable enough with one-who-saws to use our private language. It's like intuitively you know he's worthy, like of being in our inner circle. Her Royal Highness Bower would call this *foreshadowing*." Bower is our English teacher. Bower resembles the Queen of England.

"Shit," I say. "As usual, you are probably right. Was it obvious I liked him?"

"To me. Not to him," Kale says. "You forget how clueless guys are."

"Shit," I say again.

"Ca-ca," says Kale. Now she is onto terms for fecal matter. We found a list of these once in a psychology textbook in my dad's office.

"Boom-boom," I say.

"Double boom-boom," says Kale.

"Boom-boom is already double. That, Bower would so kindly inform you, is *redundant*."

"Alas," says Kale. "So put me in grammar prison."

Everyone mocks our English teacher, but Kale and I secretly revere her. Bower is old, older than you would think for someone still teaching high school. She's short and has a small build, white hair, and glasses. Kids call her "Old Lady

Bower" and because she doesn't wear a wedding ring, they make jokes about how she's the seventy-year-old virgin. But they should shut up, because no one knows 1) how old she is; or 2) anything about her life outside of school. She could easily be divorced or widowed. Or maybe a lesbian. She could've had plenty of sex in her life whether she was married or not, gay or straight. The thing is, she doesn't have to explain herself to any of us and that's one thing that makes her formidable. She's wicked smart about literature and doesn't have to answer to any dumb teenager.

"When I go home, I need to recommit to my goals," I say.

We're quiet after that, lying on our backs, side by side on her mom's old sheet. The sun is high and feels good beating down on me. I imagine the heat and the sweat as cleansing. By lying here, I'm purifying. And then, as always when I'm left with my own thoughts, I think of my mother and I wonder if, wherever she is, she can see me down here. Like Google Earth, just zoom right in on me from her celestial place. Does she know what I think? That I have a crush on this swimmer boy? That I'm sorry in a thousand different ways?

Kale is putting on her shirt, standing up to step into her shorts. "I'm hungry," she says. "Come on, we can go to the restaurant and I'll share my free meal with you."

She gets one free meal per shift at the vegetarian Mexican place on Duval—Mother's Café. She's the counter person and the smoothie maker and the one who does fruit salads and carrot juice. She has been helping the owner/manager develop vegan items for the menu. That's how Kale is. The youngest employee there and she's making changes to the menu.

"Yum," I say. "Can we do the vegan nachos? Or the spinach enchiladas?"

"Whatever you want, but we have to hurry because we

have to bike across town, order, eat, and then I have to go home and shower and change."

As we make the long trek back to where our bikes are locked in the parking lot, I scan the pool for Swimmer Boy-Who-Saws. The place is in full swing now—moms and kids and no school and long lazy days. It is nearly impossible to find someone—Barton Springs is huge. But I make a wish to see him one more time before I leave, and then there he is—shallow section, far away—green swim trunks and a half-dozen kids in a semi-circle around him.

"Look," I say to Kale.

"What?"

"One-who-saws." I point.

"There are a hundred people where you're pointing, Tate."

"Green shorts, bare chest, encircled by children."

"Got it," she says. "He's cute."

"And sweet," I add, "with that gaggle of kids always following him."

"Ducklings."

"Exactly. Or goslings."

"Goslings it is," says Kale. "Goslings is a far superior word." She grabs my arm and pulls. "We have to hurry."

"So he has another name," I say. "Mother Goose."

"And one-who-saws," she says. She's unlocking our bikes, which are hooked together.

"And one-who-swims, AKA Swimmer Boy."

She untangles her bike from the rack and gives me the look: we're in a hurry. I get serious, grab my steed, and jump on.

The ride from south Austin to Hyde Park takes a good half hour, but we are fast. The exercise feels great, the steady pumping of the pedals, the hot humid wind in my hair, the satisfaction of propelling myself forward with my own power.

Kale sets the pace. Her dark curls trail out behind her like streamers from her helmet.

As we pass downtown, the capitol building, and head up through the university, I'm reminded that my poor sweet father is sitting in that courtroom, probably right now, with his lawyer and the lawyer's assistants, and they are doing their best to defend him against a crime he is psychologically incapable of committing. At some point, they'll call me as a witness. The lawyer (one who laws?) says it could be many months or even as long as a year. I am the kind of witness the defense saves for when they really need me. I try to send my dad a good vibe as I cruise past. My thoughts turn to Swimmer Boy, Sawyer, what a nice name, and then to nachos, and back and forth, equally delicious.

CHAPTER THREE:

JUST WHEN SHE WAS BEGINNING...

Greta's in town, partly to attend a few days of the trial, mostly to take me camping. She's my aunt on my mom's side and we have gone camping every summer since I was eleven. Well, except last summer, when no one was in the mood. Last summer is a total blur.

Greta is staying in the main house until we leave for the Grand Canyon, but she's the one adult who would be welcome to stay in my studio. She's more like a friend or a sister than an aunt. More like me than like Carla, her own sister. But there are three bedrooms in the big house and she wants to give me my space.

She knocks after she gets home from court. I'm looking at colleges on the internet.

"Entré," I say.

"Hola," she says. "How goes it?"

"Check this out." She looks over my shoulder. "These five

colleges are all grouped together into something called the EcoLeague. Basically, if you get accepted into one of them, it's an acceptance into all five."

"Cool," Greta says. "Look at the one in Vermont—Green Mountain College—that just sounds fun. And look—that one in Arizona isn't far from where we're going camping."

"You mean we could maybe check it out?"

"I don't see why not. Leave the canyon a day early, go there, get a hotel. You should call them and let them know you're coming. Get an appointment."

While I type an email to their admissions office, Greta browses around the room.

"I like your goals," she says. "I should get mine big like that. More in-your-face. I put mine on little Post-it notes and then I wonder why I lose them."

I turn to look at the goal poster with her.

"Number four is about to be crossed off," I say.

"And if we go see that school in Arizona, we're accomplishing part of number three," Greta says. "NO WAY!"

"What?"

"Number ten! I just ordered you a vegan cookbook! It should be here tomorrow."

"Read my mind."

"I figured we'd need help with camping food you could eat."

"Camping vegan is simple. Most of what people bring camping is already vegan—trail mix, peanut butter, power bars…"

"Beef jerky," says Greta.

I give her a look. "The cookbook will be good for making something nice at home. Maybe I'll have someone over for dinner."

"Maybe some lucky guy," Greta says.

"Have you not read number six?"

"Oh yeah, number six," Greta says. "Swearing off boys forever? That seems extreme."

"No, not forever. *Till I get my act together.* Can you not read anymore?"

"Well," says Greta, "in my opinion, not that anyone's asking for it, you have your act together way more than most people I know, and people much older than you, too."

"That's your opinion, Garbo. I'll take it into consideration." There was once a famous actress named Greta Garbo.

"Jasper is a dunce," says Garbo, out of nowhere.

"Where did *that* come from?"

"I know it's been a year, but I still think it sucks the biggest weenie that a guy would bail on you right when you need him most. Good riddance."

"He's an okay guy," I say. "He just couldn't handle it. I'm sure his parents weren't overjoyed to have their son dating the girl who..."

Greta interrupts: "Yeah, but none of that was your fault. Anyway, what I'm saying is there's someone better out there for you. And, I think you're wise beyond your years to know that now's not the best time to go out boy-shopping."

"Exactly."

At Greta's favorite Mexican place, she eats a chili relleno oozing with cheese and I have my first wave of doubt about being vegan. My former favorite food? Pizza. Second place: grilled cheese and tomato sandwiches. Third place: mac and cheese. I'm having the corn tamale and salad. But damn, her cheese looks good.

"Should I have a bite of that?" I say.

"If you want."

"I'm not eating cheese," I remind her, indignant.

"Well, I know, nut job. I'm just saying if you want a bite

of my food, it's yours."

"I don't. I just had to entertain the idea...nut job."

"The nut job is you." Greta takes another bite and the cheese hangs off her fork in strings.

"Is it good?" I say.

"Not gonna answer that."

"Come on. Is it delicious?"

"No, it's completely icky and I'm gonna go make myself barf," she says. "Yes, it is utterly, exquisitely fantastic. Otherwise, I would not order it every time I come here."

"Just checking," I say.

"Sooooo..." she says, in a way that I know means she's about to 1) change the subject; and 2) bring up something difficult.

"Sooooo..." I say back to her.

"I noticed in your ten goals, there was the one about helping your dad through all this, but there was nothing about your mom."

"Can't exactly help her *now*."

"Well," Greta says, "it's not the same as what you might do for your dad, obviously, because she's not here, but it seems weird to completely leave her off the list."

"The list is for goals. Get a job. Look at schools." I take the last bite of my tamale and wipe up the rest of the salsa with it.

"I know. I think they're great goals—I already said that. I just wondered if there was anything you wanted to do around the loss of your mom."

"Such as? And please don't say therapy."

"I don't know. Hell, I should let you handle it your way and figure out my own stuff. The truth is, I need to do something myself. Not that Carla and I were even close, because we weren't. But I lost a sister, in a horrible, unfair, brutal way, and I don't know what to do about it."

"Trial's got to you?"

"And that woman from *48 Hours*. She grilled me throughout the afternoon recess."

"You *talked* to her?!"

"Listen to you! You watch those shows constantly. Correction: obsessively."

"Watching is one thing. But talking to them? What did you say?"

Greta wipes salt from the empty chip bowl with her finger and licks it off.

"I said Carla had been a very troubled person for most of her adult life. And I said it was particularly tragic that just when she was beginning to turn her life around, someone took it from her." Greta's voice trails off in my mind, as I choose instead to focus on the mariachi music, the superbright tablecloths, the sombreros on the wall.

"Can we go?" I say. "I want to stop at Home Depot to look at shelves for the studio."

Greta wipes her mouth with a paper napkin she's been shredding in her lap. The waiter never took away the other two place settings at our four-top, so I unroll one of the silverware sets and pass Greta a new napkin.

"Thanks," she says and looks at the former napkin, barely there. She laughs. "That's pathetic," she says.

"You decimate things," I tell her. "Look at the label from your beer bottle."

She has peeled off the label, torn it into strips, and twisted each strip between two fingers until the strip of paper is a mere pellet.

"I do, don't I?"

"Nervous?" I say.

Greta says, "Sad, frustrated, confused."

"Don't forget angry. According to everything they have

me read, we are supposed to be very, very angry." The waiter drops off our check. "No flan this time?" he says. We both shake our heads. Usually Greta gets flan and I get Mexican hot chocolate. We both make the universal sign for "full" by touching our bellies.

"Angry?" Greta says when he leaves. "We're still supposed to be angry?"

"Apparently. Until you get really angry, you haven't even begun to deal with it."

"Are you?" Greta asks.

"Mostly at myself. For not speaking to Carla for pretty much the last two years of her life."

"God, Tate, I know, but she was not easy, and plenty of girls your age fight with their moms over so much less, over nothing. You had no way of knowing her days on the planet were numbered."

"True. But it still makes me angry." I turn the empty chip bowl over and perch the salt and pepper shakers on top, like a bride and groom on a wedding cake. The pepper is the guy.

"You referred to her as Carla."

"Yeah?"

"Not Mom?"

"I haven't called her Mom for a long time."

CHAPTER FOUR:

THE STATUS QUO

They should've had me on their list of suspects. It's the first thing Homicide looks for on all the shows: was there anyone who was angry with the deceased? Any spurned lover or lunatic landlord or irate employee? Anyone she'd recently pissed off? Anyone with a motive?

Not that I would ever kill someone; I'd relocate ants that get inside the kitchen before I'd step on them. But in terms of someone having a motive—she and I did *not* get along.

Funny thing was, they investigated Jasper. What a joke. I guess they thought that a teenage girl having trouble with her mom would incite her beau to do the dirty work. Jasper heads up a group at school called Nonviolent Communicators. They do volunteer mediation sessions in town. His mom and dad are Quakers. If there's anyone less likely than me or my dad to harm someone physically, that would be Jasper. So it was humorous, only at the time I wasn't laughing. They questioned Jasper only two days after. That time period is like thick fog in my head.

They ruled him out as a suspect immediately, but they never even questioned me.

I always think of this when I'm waiting to get in to see Dad. There are certain times you can visit and no matter how often you go, each time they put you through the same rigmarole and search. I'm allowed to bring my dad his favorite sandwich—meatloaf on pumpernickel with spicy mustard— but every single time they're going to open the sandwich. And look through my backpack, and frisk me. Usually that's what the wait is—getting a female guard to come pat me down. They all know me by now. It's evident they feel sorry for me, and I end up acting extra chipper and upbeat in the hopes of convincing them all is cool. Contrary to popular belief, folks, I am not the most pitiable creature on the planet. Take the endangered sea turtle, for instance. The mother comes out of the water to lay her eggs on the beach and then leaves them there, untended. Sometimes the eggs are stolen by poachers and served up at restaurants as a delicacy. Other times, cars run over the nest, smashing the eggs. The lucky babies who do hatch must fend for themselves by making their way to the water. Instinctively, they go toward the brightest horizon, responding to reflected light. These days, street lights, headlights, and even flashlight beams can throw them off course. They need the reflected natural light of the moon. The sea turtle is clumsy on land, and doesn't see well. The babies have trouble if, in between the nest where they've hatched and their future ocean home, they fall into the deep rut of a tire track, or even a moat some kid dug around his sand castle. Often once this happens, they don't find their way out. They can die, mere moments after they've hatched. What kind of a mom leaves her babies to find their own way like that?

Once I'm in, it's a series of locked doors and then we sit at a table together, Dad and me, no clear panel between us like you've seen on TV shows, where the two people have to talk on phones, even though they are looking right at each other. Even the guards seem puzzled by why my father's the best they could come up with in this case.

Here are the reasons I know he's innocent. 1) He is Mr. Completely Calm about everything, to a fault. I love the man, but he could try to get mad about something, anything, once in a while. He used to let Carla treat him like crap. Dad was always the mature, stable, reliable partner and parent, since day one. 2) He is a psychologist, a licensed child and family counselor, and has taught counseling at the local community college. And 3) A good ten years ago, he started a non-profit called the Center for the Family. Counseling and mediation services donated by local practitioners, so that even low income folks could aspire to better family relationships. He even got a big grant to do it. So you can imagine how the media went to town with this. Esteemed family counselor, head of Austin's groundbreaking Center for the Family, murders ex-wife. I mean you tell me, what is wrong with this picture? He is not capable of this ire or this act. (In the vocab part of our English class, Bower taught us the word *ire*. Comes from the same root as *irate*, *irritate*, *irascible*.)

There are stories to corroborate my father's overly calm and collected demeanor even under pressure. Carla (AKA my mother) often told me things she shouldn't have. She told me that during her many affairs, she was meeting the next door neighbor, Frank, on his lunch hour. His wife and kids had gone to visit the grandparents in Milwaukee. They were having a rendezvous—my mom said Frank liked to call it a "nooner" and she preferred the term "Afternoon Delight" but whatever—they were two married people having sex in the daytime, in his house.

My dad decided that day to surprise my mom—she'd been blue and feeling trapped, having to stay home all the time with the baby (*moi*). So he picked up eggrolls and combination lo mein at her favorite Chinese place and drove to the house. This was when we lived in Illinois.

Her car was in the garage; the door was unlocked. I was asleep in the crib upstairs.

But his wife was nowhere to be found.

Now here comes the good part, so pay attention. My dad has intuition from all his years peering into people's psychologies. He knows that everyone next door is out-of-town except for Frank. And he knows Frank has cheated on his wife before, because his wife went to my dad for counseling. So he puts two and two together, walks the short distance to the neighbors', sees Frank's car. He stands and listens for a minute on the front step, tries the door, and finds it open. He walks inside their house. (He may not have a temper, but the man's got balls.)

When Carla told me this story, I was maybe eight years old and she told it in this suspenseful way, like I was supposed to derive great narrative pleasure out of the tale. She did not get, for a second, that it was 1) a story that painted her in a very bad light; and 2) not exactly an age-appropriate tale for her young daughter. I don't think Dr. Seuss has covered that one: *Hop On Anyone's Pop; The Grinch Who Stole Fidelity; Every Who Down in Whoville has Slept with My Mom.*

My father hears action upstairs, but he's not stupid enough to explore. He just calls out, "Carla, are you up there?" She said she considered jumping out the window and dashing back to the house, pretending she'd been in the bathroom, but she looked and it was a long way down, and she was buck naked.

She and Frank froze, and my father said, "Come on home now, Carla." And left.

She said she showed up soon after, and Dad gave her a

lecture, said he treated her more like a teenager who was acting out than like a wife having an affair. He didn't seem jealous—just annoyed. "We're married, Carla," he said. "Married people don't behave this way."

She felt like a kid being grounded. She refused the Chinese take-out and Dad went back to work. That made me so sad, how my dad's idea of the take-out backfired.

Carla used to enjoy telling me these adventure stories— the close calls and the times she got caught in the act. My dad has never been anything but patient and tolerant. With her. With me.

I guess most kids go through times when they feel closer to one parent than the other. For some, maybe the allegiance goes back and forth. But for me, it's always been my dad. As early as I can remember, he was the one I sought out. When I fell off my bike, when I lost my goldfish down the drain, when some pea-brain was mean to me after school, it was Dad I went to for help, for answers, for comfort. Carla could be comforting, too. I remember her putting aloe on my back and shoulders once when I got a brutal sunburn. Of course, the sunburn itself was her fault—my dad couldn't believe she'd forgotten something as crucial as sunscreen. We were at the pool all day. She lathered me up good at first, but after I swam it was all gone. She was drinking wine coolers that afternoon, from a small ice chest. She was reading a magazine. To her credit, when she saw how burned I was getting, she made me put on my long-sleeved t-shirt. It's a good memory, though. Not the burn or the itching or the way my skin peeled off in strips a week later—but the two nights when she put layer after layer of cool aloe on my back. Something about a mother's hand, her fingers. The circular motion, the spiral, the pads of her fingertips.

Carla cut hair, though she could have done anything.

When I was little, I thought the whole beauty parlor thing was cool—the chair that could be pumped up and down, the plastic cape to keep the hair off your clothes, the dye charts and the dryers and the hair magazines everywhere. You'd pick how you wanted to look and Carla could usually pull it off. She had customers who'd been going to her for years.

Later, though, when I was ten, eleven, twelve, I would think of beauty school, cosmetology school, and I'd cringe. A lot of my friends had professional moms. Kale's mom, for instance—an OB/GYN. I started to feel embarrassed about Carla's job.

Then there were her boyfriends, even before the divorce. She was constantly sleeping with someone. On the nights the custody agreement mandated I sleep at her place, she would have guys over. They would get high or shit-faced and I would stay in my room. The next morning there was the inevitable mess and the challenge of getting her up so she could take me to school. Often, she would get the guy to drop me off and I would have to tell some man I didn't even know how to get to my school. Carla, if it was her day off, would sleep.

I was twelve when I stopped letting her cut my hair. This hurt her feelings. It was cruel. She had always given me great haircuts. I just decided I'd deny her the pleasure of touching her only daughter's hair.

At thirteen, I asked to live with my dad full-time and she stopped speaking to me.

At fourteen, she wanted to be back in my life again, but I was busy holding a grudge. A couple months later, I reconsidered, but gave her an ultimatum: quit drinking or else we don't have a relationship. She chose the "or else."

Sure, you'll say, how convenient for you to say this now, but it's true: *I was just about to give her another chance.* I kept hearing from Aunt Greta how Carla was really getting her act together. She went to AA meetings and quit drinking. She went to some other group for people who are addicted to love and sex. She started taking art classes at the community college and when she took ceramics, she was hooked. From that class forward, Carla became an artist, a ceramicist, and I'm ashamed to say I didn't find out until she was dead how talented she was. To her, it was like cutting hair. She said she always saw someone's head as a starting point and then she would sculpt their hair into something artful. With ceramics, she did it all—the wheel, hand-built stuff, big, small, thin, thick. She said cutting hair had prepared her for this new skill. She said all this to me over the phone, the first conversation I'd allowed her in all those years. Even then, I let her do all the talking, but I did listen. I heard.

I was supposed to drop by the studio behind her house where she did her work. It was actually *on my list* the same week she was killed. I'm not sure what was keeping me from going, but sometimes when someone you have decided will never change actually does, it can be a little disappointing. 1) You don't want to be wrong about something like this; 2) you don't know if you can trust the change; and 3) it's just an adjustment. You want to believe what you long ago concluded about the person: lost cause. They turn up changed for the better and you don't know what to do.

Dad was thrown off by it too, I think. We were more comfortable with the status quo. Our response to her had become habit. As much as you think you want someone to change, there's a way you come to rely on their being who they are, bad as that may be. It's familiar and something you can count on. Carla shook it all up, and it bothered us both, though we've never discussed it—how she finally changed, not for Dad and not for me, but because she found pottery and because she fell for some guy in AA, finally a guy she wanted to be faithful to.

Three days after he proposed to her and she said yes, nearly two years into our stand-off, four months before my sixteenth birthday, someone extinguished her, smashed her dead.

Did you know *bludgeon* is both a noun and a verb?

The first syllable—*bludge*—sounds like the act itself. Onomatopoeia.

That word bludgeon makes me sick.

CHAPTER FIVE:

GRAND CANYON

Greta and I are having a farting contest in the tent. There are awards for loudest and stinkiest. She's winning both.

"Damn," I say to her. "You need to cut back on the black beans."

"Need I remind you of the year I lived with your mom and dad?" she says. "I changed an indeterminate number of stinky diapers. Yours, I might add, thank you very much."

"Baby poop isn't that stinky," I tell her.

"Are you insane? It's horrendous."

Greta has issues around pooping, always has. She worries about things like when she will have to go, where she'll be, if there will be people nearby, etc. To use her own word, she is *loath* to poop in a public restroom, but if she has to, she finds airports the easiest of all public facilities. When asked why they are easier, she says something about the transience. People moving through. It's not like you'll meet up again with the woman who was in the stall next to you. She's long gone, you're long gone; you've each headed in different directions. She has a fondness for pit toilets at campgrounds because they are always off by themselves, remote and private, but she can't stand the smell. It takes her a while to do the deed. I'm so fast, I can pretty much go in, hold my breath, and get out of there before having to inhale. She envies my efficient pooping skills. I tell her it's the new vegan diet and she should try it.

I call it "snapping a deuce." Number Two—get it?

She calls it "dropping the kids off at the pool."

She says she could hardly call what she does "snapping" as that connotes something quick, as in a snap of the fingers. Dropping off kids has a lingering connotation more accurate for her. My ex-boyfriend Jasper—he and his guy friends called it "pinching a loaf" but Greta and I have ruled that one out as too disgusting—referencing poop as food—conjuring up in your head a loaf of bread, or a meat loaf, or those nasty cheese and nut loaves people have at Christmas. For that matter, fruit cake.

I remind Greta that *her* favorite saying for this equates fecal matter with *offspring*. She thinks, since she isn't a mom, this is okay.

"You'd be a good mom, though," I say.

She says thanks and tells me to go to sleep. We have a long hike tomorrow.

I used to sleep soundly when camping. I always liked the feeling of being cocooned inside a sleeping bag, and I don't mind the hard ground. I have one of those inflatable Therm-a-Rest pads and it works fine. But now, on the first camping trip since the incident, there are things to worry about after dark. I don't say anything to Greta, don't know if she's awake too, worried too, wondering like me if the man who killed my mother might be at this very campground, eager to bludgeon again. I even talk myself into thinking it makes sense—someone running from a crime *would* go to the nearest national park, crowded with a constantly changing cast of characters, total anonymity. Between me and Greta and a lunatic, there is nothing but this tent—ripstop, thin fabric. I cannot stop myself from thinking of things with which one might bludgeon. A club, a bat, a log, an axe, a boulder. The bench from the picnic table. I lie and listen, ready to leap up at the first sound of trouble.

Neither of my parents were campers or outdoor enthusiasts. But Greta took me all over. The Grand Canyon is one of the places we like to return to—this is our third time. We've done the North Rim, Havasupai Canyon, and now we're doing what most tourists do—the South Rim. We'll hike down as far as Phantom Ranch tomorrow and then back out to this same campsite the next night. I'll have to imagine this all over again, the possibility of a murderer on the loose. Sounds silly, but no one ever would've expected one in our Austin neighborhood, either. I'm ready for morning. Everything's manageable in daylight. Eventually, finally, I sleep.

Yesterday we did the quick rim trails, the little quarter-mile nature walks and vista points and visitors' center. We bought our postcards and watched the film.

Now, before heading out on the real hike, we sit in on an info session for backpackers. We learn that people hiking into the canyon in the summer need to carry a gallon of water per person per day. The ranger tells stories about people not taking this seriously. The descent is so easy, they think it won't be that bad coming back out—but it's hard and it's hot and you sweat a lot and lose water and this is the desert, for God's sake, and you need to hydrate constantly even when you're *not* doing rigorous exercise. We listen. Greta is the type to do whatever they recommend.

The ranger covers all the other dangers, like heat stroke and rattlesnake bites, like falling into the canyon. He says, "Now who do you think falls over the edge most often?" Nobody says anything. "Do you think it's children? NO, it's not children. Do you think it's elderly people? NO, the elderly follow the rules. The people who fall to their death in the Grand Canyon are typically young men, from the age of eighteen to twenty-six." One guy who fits into that age range lets out a little laugh. "WHY do they fall in?" the ranger asks. He points to that one guy, challenging him to come up with an answer. "Goofing around?" the guy says. "Exactly," says the park ranger. He explains that they are the ones most likely to go past a sign that says to stay back. They want to scramble a little on the edges; they want to lean far out there and get a better photograph; they want to impress their friends and *girlfriends* (Ranger Rick emphasizes this) by not being afraid, not heeding the silly warning signs. And the next thing you know, they're overboard. "Do NOT take these risks!" he says. "I would rather not carry you out of here in a body bag." I roll my eyes to Greta, like this guy is a real drama queen, is he not?

Greta answers my eye roll with a poke in the side—uses her elbow.

"Ow," I say. "What?"

"Pay attention to Yogi Bear."

"Yogi Bear? What are you talking about?"

"I mean Smokey the Bear. Listen to what he has to say."

Smokey opens it up to Q and A, and someone asks about rattlesnake bites.

"Slice it and suck out the venom," whispers Greta. She makes a face.

"Ick," I say.

"Not really. Don't listen to me. I have no idea."

Turns out the most likely group to get bitten by a rattle-snake is, you guessed it, young men between eighteen and twenty-four. Apparently, between twenty-four and twenty-six, some guys wise up, at least where serpents are concerned.

We leave the info session, and head back to our tent to get geared up for the hike down. Every walkway is crowded with tourists and the parking lots are filled with tour buses. People of every nationality wield cameras and water bottles. It's only nine a.m. and it's hot.

"Why are guys so stupid?" I say to Greta.

"They're just being macho. It's like birds when they plump up and fluff out their feathers to look bigger and stronger to attract the females during mating time. Like a peacock open-ing the fan of his tail up to all those glorious colors. Boys are trying to be bigger and bolder than they actually are. So they puff up, hang over the edge of the cliff, fall in. They don't know when to stop, and they don't want to be seen as chicken, and there's a lot of pressure from each other to perform in these ways."

"I can't see Dad as ever having been like that," I say.

"Me either," says Greta. "Your father is not a typical male, no way no how."

"And Jasper," I say. "He'd never hot-dog around on the edge of the Grand Canyon. He's Mr. Boy Scout."

"So that's good. You choose men who aren't afraid to be safe. They're secure enough in who they are that they don't have to take big showy risks."

"Sawyer..." I begin, then stop myself.

"Who's Sawyer?"

"This guy who taught Kale swimming lessons."

"Is he a hot-dogging type? A show-off? Macho dude?"

"Not at all."

"And why are we examining the habits of this Sawyer fellow, may I ask? This guy who taught Kale's swim class?"

"We're not examining his habits," I say. "I just think he's also the kind of guy who doesn't fit this park ranger's stereotype of the average young male."

Greta looks at me.

"What?" I say.

She just smiles.

"Stop it," I say. "We were just talking about macho behavior and I was telling you guys I know who aren't necessarily like that."

"And," says Greta, "you brought up your father, your ex-boyfriend, and this Sawyer fellow. Like, Sawyer got put in a pretty key category of men you know, that's all I'm saying."

"Yeah, so? I'm not going to be dating anyone anyway, remember?"

"I remember."

"So. End of story."

"But if you were, just hypothetically, this Sawyer guy might be of interest."

"Hypothetically speaking, perhaps."

Greta gives me a hip bump, hard, and I lose my balance and knock into the kid next to me, who nearly drops his hamburger.

"Sorry!" I say to the boy. Greta cracks up. "Are you crazy?" I say to her. "Are you trying to lose me over the edge of the canyon?" We're not even close to the edge, but I'm just messing with her.

"Right," says Greta. "You figured out my master plan. Over the edge. And then I'll never have to take you on one of these silly trips again." She rubs her hands together. "Hmmm, I wonder if there will be any insurance money."

"I want a hamburger," I say. "Like that kid had."

"So get in line. Weird breakfast, but to each her own. So

this Sawyer, is he a vegan also?"

"Not that I know of."

"Just checking."

"You can forget about him, Garbo, okay?"

"But can *you*? That is the question."

I hip bump her back when she least expects it, and she bashes into the trash can outside of the concession. The outside of the can is covered with melted ice cream and flies and bees. When she regains her balance, she runs after me, but I'm already way ahead of her. People step back to make way for our chase scene. They hold their children's shoulders, and look at us like we're nuts, or juvenile delinquents, or criminals. But we're just a girl and her aunt, having a blast. Right then, running like that, wild, at the South Rim of the Grand Canyon, I feel better than I've felt in a long time.

CHAPTER SIX:

IN A PLACE LIKE THIS

At Phantom Ranch, Greta wakes me early so we can get a head start on the hard part of this hike—the trek back up to the rim. We each have a Luna Bar and then get going. We're set for water and munchies and will get a big meal, our reward, at one of the restaurants when we finish. Greta always likes to talk about what she's craving, what she's going to order. She has a long list going of foods she misses, even though we've only been camping for three days.

"I'm already tired," she says, before we've gone a quarter-mile. "Whose idea was this? It's all uphill."

"You could've hired one of those mules," I remind her.

"I don't like the mules. Well, let me qualify that: I don't like the poopie the mules leave all over this damn trail."

"They have to poop somewhere."

"I know. I'm not blaming the mules. I'm saying I don't think people should be riding mules into the Grand Canyon. If they're too lazy to walk it, they should just stay up at the top."

"What about a handicapped person?"

Greta thinks about this. "I guess they can have a mule," she says. "But they have to be handicapped! I want card-carrying handicapped people only on the mules."

"When you're governor of the state of Arizona, you can make that rule."

"Damn straight," says Greta. "I'm going to write my campaign speech when we get back."

We're quiet for a long while. Occasionally we pass someone, or someone from behind passes us. We take frequent breaks. The backs of my calves hurt with every step and I fear my body will stick permanently in this upward-seeking angle.

Just after we pass a mile marker indicating we're halfway through the day's ascent, Greta calls for a break. "Can't believe I'm already thirsty again," she says.

We remove our packs, pull out our water bottles, and sit down just off the trail near some rocks. As I'm screwing the lid off my bottle, it slips from my hands, bounces once on the ground, and spills, turning the red sand on the ground from a coral color to a deep brick.

"Damn," I say, and right the bottle before much has escaped.

"Who needs water?" says Greta. "It's only about 110 degrees. I think I'll share some of mine with the trees and rocks also."

"Wise ass," I say. "Anyway, I didn't share mine with trees and rocks. I shared it with the earth."

"The parched earth," Greta says. She makes a weird little whining noise, like maybe the sound the earth might make if crying.

"Exactly," I say. And then the noise happens again, but I'm looking right at Greta and she's not the one making it. She looks at me, wondering the same thing.

"What in the hell?" She stands up.

"I thought that was you," I tell her.

"And I thought it was you."

And that's when we see the man curled up behind a rock. His skin is scarlet with sunburn and the slice of his leg that shows between his socks and his pants leg is scaly like a lizard. He's lying on his side, in khaki pants and a T-shirt. I would guess he's about sixty.

"Oh my God," says Greta. "Are you okay?"

The man makes the whining noise again. He points to his mouth.

"Water!" Greta says, and we both reach for our bottles.

She asks him if he can sit up to take a drink, and he does a small shake of the head. "Did you fall?" Greta says. He shakes it again. "Did you sleep here?" He makes his best attempt at a nod.

We consider how much water we'll sacrifice if we try to pour it into his mouth. Greta pulls out a bandana, one she's not used yet. She always has three, and has been known to use them as bandages, as potholders, and as a way to cool her head—wetting them down and tying them around her forehead. This one is in a side pocket of her pack, and dusty when she shakes it out. We pour a little water onto the bandana and let it soak the cloth. Then she holds it over the man's mouth and squeezes. He soaks it up as quickly as the dry ground did. He opens his mouth for more, like a bird. Greta repeats the process.

"What if he has heat stroke?" I say. "We need to get help."

"He's dehydrated."

"We need to call for help," I repeat. "But of course we don't have a phone." This has been the only source of argument on the trip. Greta has always been anti cell phones. Doesn't even own one. And she wouldn't let me carry mine in my pack—

said it went against all her instincts in the wild, to have such a thing. To imagine it ringing in the middle of nowhere. She thinks it's absurd. I gave in, as I always do on the phone issue, realizing that these days, at a place as popular as this canyon, if we were to need a phone, someone would come by before long who would have one. But now that we are in a situation where we clearly need one, I'm burning mad and Greta can tell. She's holding the man's head up now so that he can get big sips. In between, she's trying to get him to answer questions. I fume.

"Relax, Tate."

"Relax?"

"One of us can run ahead for help."

"Oh, that should be really expeditious," I say. "Have you not noticed our snail's pace?"

"What do you suggest, Tate?" she says. "Tell me what you're thinking."

"I'm thinking what I always think! That we should have a phone! Everybody would have a phone. You're living in the dark ages, Garbo! This is one of those things that separates you from all the parents in the world. A parent, *any* parent, would have a phone! They just would! I mean, have you ever heard of Safety First? Like, what if one of us were to break a leg?"

Greta, eternally calm and clear-headed, just looks at me. She gets an expression on her face that I've seen enough times to know she's moving into concerned mode—instead of getting pissed back at me, she's worried about me. I don't want her concern; I want her to fight back. She is reminding me of my father. Did everyone who ever hung around with Carla have to adopt this steadiness, so that Carla could be the wacko one?

"Am I right?" I say. I'm determined to make my point.

"You're right about parents and phones," she says.

"So why do you insist on never bringing a phone, even when it makes total sense? I mean, you follow the recommended amounts of water to a T, but you won't dream of having a way to call for help?" I look at the man again, whose eyes are shut. He looks so small and vulnerable there, in fetal position."Well?" I say.

"What?"

"Why are you so stubborn about the damn cell phone thing?" I'm yelling, and the look I'm giving her could burn holes through travertine.

I feel some emotion coming large up my throat, burning behind my eyes, threatening to turn into tears. "And meanwhile," I say, my voice starting to shake, "the lunatic who crushed my mom's head still walks around...the fucker is free...he could be here, for all we know." I can't hold it back and I'm crying hard, in jagged sobs. Greta reaches to put an arm around me and I slough her off.

"Hey!" A man has just come around the bend with what looks like his wife and son. "What's the trouble? Can we help?"

Greta shows him the old man, and he goes into action. He checks his vitals and inside his mouth. He tells his wife to go up or down the trail until she gets a signal and to call the emergency number. Each of them, even the young boy, has a phone out and ready.

"He's stable," the man tells us. "You did the right thing, getting some water into him." He looks at me. "He your grandpa?"

I shake my head.

"Relative?"

I look at Greta, like *fix this*. Like *don't make me talk when I'm like this*.

"We don't know the man," she says. "We just came across

him. My niece is upset about something else."

"My *aunt*," I say, "has something against cell phones." I say it mean.

The man looks at me like *is that what you're crying about? A phone?* And I don't care what he or anyone else thinks. He stays by the old man, tells him help is on the way. The wife and son have given us all some room. They are seated just off the trail up ahead. The emergency has been reported and the woman has a bag of pecans out, and the boy unwraps a fruit roll-up. Fruit roll-ups remind me of my mother—I mean Carla—something she used to put in my lunch box. I force another surge of sadness away, using the same will that kept me walking up the ridiculously cruel incline of this ridiculously deep canyon. Tears sting at the rims of my eyes, but they don't spill. They pool there and the dry world around me drinks them up. A person could lose a lot of tears in a place like this.

Greta pulls some food out of her pack, and I sit down right where I am, looking out over the gigantic expanse. It's weird how a landscape this dry can sometimes trick you into thinking it's wet. Like when you're driving a long, straight shot of road, and you'll see up ahead what looks like a shallow puddle, but when you arrive at the puddle, it's disappeared, a mirage. Here in the Grand Canyon in the summer, heat waves hover above some surfaces. There's something watery about them. Part of me wants to leap out into the void, and find those heat waves shimmering there like the surface of a vertical lake. I bet out there, where the water is imaginary, I could find my buoyancy easily.

I focus on the clouds, the cliffs, and the nothingness between them. In front of me, up close, I focus on some kind of cactus, asserting itself from a sharp crack in the rock. I don't know what kind it is, but I make a mental note of its shape and size so I can look it up later. It's a hardy-looking thing—mean almost, but out here, you have to be if you're going to survive.

CHAPTER SEVEN:

SOME TIDAL WAVE

In the next half hour, Greta needs me to make up my mind about visiting that Eco League college. She doesn't care either way (but really she does—she's big on education), but if we're going, she needs to turn off at the next exit. Greta doesn't hesitate to say she *thinks* we should stick with the plan—we allowed time for the side trip, she reminds me, and we have an appointment. But she'll leave it up to me. What it all boils down to is that Greta's worried about me. The incident with the old man put a damper on our trip and my mood.

They evacuated him and hydrated him and gave him whatever treatment you give to someone who is drying up from the inside. They contacted his family—someone's coming to get him tomorrow. He will likely be fine. We had planned to go out for a celebratory meal after our hike back up to the rim, but I wasn't feeling that chipper so we just picked up some snacks and ate them at our campsite. The restaurant meal would've meant a shower, putting on something nice, making ourselves look presentable. When I feel this way, I lose all desire for the most basic personal grooming. I can go days without washing my hair or shaving my legs, wearing the same threadbare PJs day after day. I have at times committed the cardinal sin of going to bed without brushing my teeth, much less flossing. Greta knows this pattern and sees I'm sinking into it. She prefers to see me fight it. But it's like some tidal wave and you have to surrender, let it crash on you and push you down into a dark underworld where forms are blurry and sounds are muffled. A place where you could happily drown. A place where you could start a new life as a colorful fish, or a sea turtle.

"Two miles," Greta says, pulling me back. "Till the exit."

I know this. I saw the same sign she did. I am not blind.

Greta says, "What's it gonna be?"

"Just keep going," I say.

"Skip the Prescott College thing?"

I don't confirm or deny, because it should be obvious: yes, that's what I meant.

Greta says, "You sure? It could be fun. Get your mind off things."

If there's one thing that bugs me about Greta, it's how she keeps being nice to me when I am not being nice to her. I am silent. Get my mind off things? Well, those things always come back, stronger than ever.

The exit comes and goes. We pass the road that would've taken us to Prescott, which would've connected us to Highway 69, which normally Greta and I would snort about—a highway named after a sexual position. Greta says, "Well, I guess that's that." She makes me call the Admissions Office to tell them I'm not coming. My cell phone is still in the glove compartment and I realize I haven't even checked my voicemails. That's how funked out I am. It lights up reliably when I open it, looking odd somehow, after a few days of not seeing it. Two voicemails. The first is Kale: *Top of the mornin' to you, Tater Chip. Just wondering when you're getting back. Hope you didn't fall in. I would miss you if you did. Au Revoir. Call me. Toodles and regards to the fam.*

The second is from Big Brothers Big Sisters, a woman's voice, telling me about the upcoming training for new volunteers. New "Bigs" is what she says.

Just hearing Kale being her goofy self, and realizing I have the Big Sister thing to look forward to elevates my mood a smidgen. When Greta and I get back, no matter how late at night or how early in the morning, I can call Kale and she will rush over to see me. We will say *Salutations* and *Ta-ta* and cook up something gooey she's invented with vegan cheese.

My mind goes back to colleges. This is a big decision, I know that. I wonder if Kale and I will get to go to the same school, maybe even be roommates. Kale thinks she might like to major in literature. Bower showed us stuff we would never have seen if she didn't point it out to us, like the billboard for the optometrist in *The Great Gatsby*. She told us that big billboard with a pair of spectacles on it is like the eyes of God, watching over everything that goes on in that book with those characters. Kale and I thought that was the coolest thing.

For a second I almost tell Greta to turn the car around. *We can go to that school—it won't take long, they're expecting us after all.* It would be so easy to just change my mind. But Greta is telling me to look in the pocket on her purse for the phone number of the admissions guy.

I find it, press the numbers into my phone, and then hang up.

"What?" she says.

"Will you do it?"

"No." She has a thing about cell phones and driving, but I know in this instance, it has more to do with the fact that this was my decision, so I can deal with the consequences. Garbo is *muy* predictable in her behavior. I can read her like a book.

"I'm not sure what I should say."

"Just tell him you have to cancel our appointment. And you're sorry for the inconvenience."

I dial the number again and someone named Tony answers. He's cheerful. He's in the business of luring students.

I say I'm Tate McCoy, and we had an appointment this afternoon and we're not going to be able to make it. He says he is sorry to hear that.

"Something came up," I say. I hate lying.

After I hang up, Greta says, "Good. That's done."

"Are you mad?"

Greta shakes her head. "Nope," she says. "I'm not the one looking for a college. You'll do it when you want to do it."

I snap the phone shut and put it back into the glove.

"In that case, can I drive?"

Greta pulls over and we walk around the back of the car and slap each other five, which is what we've done each time we've changed drivers on this trip. I get in, buckle my seat-belt, adjust the seat a little closer, check all my mirrors and wait for a break in the traffic. Three eighteen-wheelers blast by, each giving the little Honda a shake. After that, there's a big gap before the next cars will reach us. I hit the gas and ease us out into the ample space.

CHAPTER EIGHT:

PAST TENSE

I'm at Big Brothers Big Sisters, waiting for my training to begin. As soon as I'm official, I will get a badge and a kid. This was one of the ideas my therapist came up with when I told her I wanted to do some volunteer work. I picked Big Brothers Big Sisters because 1) I have always wanted a brother or a sister, but never so much as now; 2) the kids who are the "littles" desperately need positive older people in their lives; and 3) my therapist's main point—it will get my mind off my own family stuff. Carla's gone, my dad's held up in the justice system—I might as well reach out to some kid who's likely seen way more trouble in life than I have.

I wanted a little brother, but they will only assign me to a girl, because I am a girl. Weird rule, and one I'll try to change if I am ever in a position of power in this organization. It's not that I won't love having a little sister, it's just that if I could choose, since I'm a girl, I'd like to get to know a brother. Like, if my parents had had two kids instead of just me, they might've wanted one of each. That sort of thing.

There are specific and sometimes funny guidelines for

how much time you spend with your little, what kinds of things you do, how much money you can or can't spend, why it's best at first not to invite a friend or family member along for activities with your little, etc. There's a screening process, which includes a background check. They don't want any pedophiles or other weirdos messing these kids up more than they are already. To make sure you're committed, they ask you to pay for the background check, which is thirty bucks—not a small amount of money for someone who has no working parent and no job. But it's a good cause, and I see why they want people to pay. Also, it keeps people who might have something sketchy in their background check from proceeding. Who's going to pay thirty bucks to have his worst secrets revealed? I take the money out of the account my grandparents on Dad's side have been saving for me. It's a college fund, but I'm allowed to take out for things like this.

The room is like a small classroom, a handful of us sitting around a long table. "Bigs," they call us. You'd think they could come up with better terminology so as not to offend people who are overweight. This is the kind of thing Kale would think about, I realize, and I send her a psychic message to get off my brainwaves. There will be two trainers, one male and one female, since there are apparently different things to learn if you're a Big Sis or a Big Bro. We're waiting for three more volunteers to show up. The woman gave us some paperwork and collected our checks and left us here in silence.

We filled out HELLO, MY NAME IS _____ stickers, so my name is out there for all to see. Of course the others around the table recognize it—there's no one in this town who hasn't heard of Carla McCoy, allegedly killed by Arthur McCoy, and their unfortunate daughter, Tate. It's not like I can pretend I'm someone else. *Oh, that poor girl? The one whose life was ruined? That's some other Tate McCoy.*

The woman trainer lets two more people into the room. Multiply the silence and awkwardness times two more bodies. Some people look down at their forms. Some look at the clock on the wall. I try to make eye contact with someone, anyone, and I exchange a look with a Mexican woman. She smiles and I smile back.

"I like your shirt," I say to her. People look up, like by breaking the silence I've broken a rule we don't even know yet.

"Thank you," she says. "It is from Oaxaca." The shirt has tiny intricate animals embroidered on it, all different colors. I should put Oaxaca on my list of places I want to go.

People eyeball my name sticker. *Yup, boys and girls, it's the famous Tate McCoy of the murdered mother! Line up to see her in person.* We are waiting for one more person. I figure if they're not going to give us something to talk about, I'll bring up a topic.

"Sooooo…" I begin, sounding like Greta. "Maybe we could all say why we've decided to volunteer."

The Mexican woman nods and says, "I like your idea. I can begin?" Her name tag says *Carlita J.*

"Go for it, Carlita," I say.

"My English is not so perfect. Excuse me. My family is in southern Mejico? Big family—three brothers and five sisters. I am *solamente*—only?—one in my family to live in United States. My husband better job in Tejas."

"You must miss all of your sisters and brothers!" I say, to help her out.

"Si," she says, and sighs. "Gracias."

"So you want to volunteer for Big Brothers Big Sisters because you want a sister locally. Nearby," I add, in case she doesn't know *local. Loco* means crazy, I know that. Don't want her to think I'm saying she wants a crazy sister.

"Yes," she says. "Thank you."

"Well," I say, "that's a good segue for me, because I have a similar reason, but different circumstances. I am an only child. *Solamente*. I've always wanted a sibling. I think I could be a really good big sister to someone who needs some help."

The large guy in the corner speaks up: "I guess you can relate to needing help, what you've been through."

Well, leave it to this dude to put it out there on the table. I'd like to disappear into some ungrammatical Spanish at this point—*Que? No comprende. Me solamente loca chica*—but instead I nod and say, "You got that right."

This brings us all back to the silence we started with. Thankfully, the door opens, and in comes the woman trainer, and lo and behold, behind her, the guy trainer... guess who?

Sawyer looks at me, and it's clear that he knew, probably from some list of names, that I would be in this room. I'm the one left to gasp like a fish. He acknowledges my surprise with a little nod and a smile. He's wearing a Big Brothers Big Sisters of Austin T-shirt. I know what he looks like under that shirt.

"One who swims," I say, and everyone looks at me and then at Carlita, like this is part of our Spanish/English dance.

"Now," says the woman trainer, whose name tag says MAGS.

"Did I miss something?" says the large man, the one I was worried about when they called us "Bigs." He looks back and forth from Sawyer to me.

"We know each other," I say to him, this hefty man who wants to get all my facts out in the open. "But I don't know your name yet."

"Joseph," he says, and scrawls onto his sticker with a black Sharpie. When he peels off the backing and sticks it over his heart, it says only Joe.

"Hi Joe. I'm Tate."

"And I'm Sawyer," says Swimmer Boy.

"I am Carlita?" says my Mexican amiga.

"Hey," says a guy labeled Rob, "this is sorta like an AA meeting."

I laugh. "I'm Tate and I am not an alcoholic." But oh, the things I could tell them about my mother.

Mags is losing her patience. "People!" she says. "We've got a lot to cover here."

On the way home from the training, I stop in to see my dad. It's been at least a week, and when I see him before he sees me, he seems down. Who wouldn't be? He has lost thirteen months of his life to this.

"There's my girl," he says when he looks up.

"I officially have a sibling." I show him my badge.

"Good deal," he says.

"Her name is Maddie. Short for Madoline. She's eight."

"How'd it go? Did you hit it off?"

"Oh, we haven't met yet. That's next. Today was just training and finding out who your 'little' is."

"Your mother and I tried to give you a sibling, you knew that right?"

"I did. Carla told me. She used to tell me everything, even stuff I did not want to hear."

"Well," Dad says, "there's nothing inappropriate about telling you we were trying to have another baby. But in other situations, she did not always exhibit the best judgment."

"That's for sure."

"Have you kept abreast of the trial?" he asks. I can't tell him how hard it is for me to dwell on it.

"I usually look at the court record online, but I haven't in a while."

"Well, you've not missed much. They have nothing definitive, the prosecution. And it goes on and on, but the progress, even on a weekly basis, seems nonexistent."

"Well, you're a trooper," I say, "for hanging in there."

"Anyway, I've lost faith in the judicial system, but that's old news," he says. "How's my favorite daughter?"

"*Only* daughter," I say, and in my head I translate: *solamente hija*, or is it *hija solamente*? "I'm doing okay, Dad."

"It kills me, sweetheart, that you have to go through this. What a nightmare."

"Trust me," I say. "You've got it much worse."

"We're both living a nightmare, different versions," he says.

"I'll be relieved when they find out who did this to Mom, and to see you out of here, but meanwhile, I'm doing what you and Mom would both want me to do—trying to go on with my life."

"Whoa. You called her Mom. Twice."

"I think I'm over that whole thing," I tell him, a little embarrassed. "She disappointed me, but she is my mother. It's biological fact."

"*Was your mother*," he says.

"Right."

It's not until I'm riding my bike home that it starts to bother me, what he said. The line keeps playing in my head. *Was your mother*. Like undue emphasis on the past tense, and contradictory to what he told me throughout the first weeks after she was killed: *she will always be your mother*. It was repeated so often it was like a mantra. Now, when I realize I should just call her Mom already, he takes this other stance? It's like as soon as I loosen my grip on a long-held grudge, he wants to hold it for me.

And the other thing I can't stop thinking about: Sawyer!

In his Big Brothers staff T-shirt. It's like everything I'm aiming to do this summer, he's already done it, and everywhere I turn, there he is, waiting for me. How am I supposed to honor Goal #6 when this boy, this swimming, sawing boy, is so omnipresent?

That night when *Dateline* comes on, I do the usual—make popcorn, melt butter, and settle on the love seat. This one is about a woman who killed her husband—he was a pastor. The congregation is shocked. But it comes out in court that he used to make her dress up and do weird things with sex. Made her watch porn and wear wigs and costumes and spike heels. They bring in one of the shoes to the courtroom as Exhibit A, and all they do is take it out of the brown bag and the defendant begins to cry. I come to the same conclusion I always do with these shows: so, maybe the guy was mean, a monster even, hiding behind his church-job-holiness in public, but in private, a real dick. Even so, does he deserve to die? Is this her only option? Does she see no other way out than to kill him? What's worse: the prison of that marriage or the actual prison where she'll spend the rest of her life? She leaves one bad situation for a worse one. Flawed logic, if you ask me. But no one asks me, so I turn off the TV, run water in the buttery bowl, and brush my teeth.

Strange the things we remember sometimes. I remember my mom teaching me how to brush my teeth. She would do it for me, but it tickled. So she said I could do it myself, and showed me why up and down is better, and why you don't brush horizontally, and how you could do your tongue at the end. Every single time I brush my teeth, this goes through my head. This basic life lesson at age three, from my mom.

CHAPTER NINE:

MAYBE

Kale makes the call for me, which is so junior high, but I don't care. I can't do it. We're in her room, 10:30 on a Friday night, after her shift at the restaurant. I'm sleeping over.

"Hey," she says into her phone.

"Yeah, hope I didn't wake you or anything." I'm only hearing her side of this conversation, because she refused to put it on speaker phone. She said if she was making the call, she was going to do it her way. Kale thinks speaker phone is rude.

"Good. Everything's great. Hey, Tate decided she wants to take you up on the private swim lessons."

"Yeah, cool, so what time?"

Then Kale says *perfect*, and *thanks*, and hangs up.

"So?"

"So, you're on. Tuesday, nine a.m., meet at the concession stand."

"What'd he say?"

"What I just told you."

"But what else did he say?"

"He said hello, he asked how it was going, we talked about

the lessons and that was pretty much it. Why are you being a weirdo?"

"I'm not. People say things between the lines, so I'm asking, did you pick up anything in the voice or manner or verbiage from one-who-swims that you would like to share with me?"

Kale says, "He sounded how he usually sounds. Sort of matter of fact."

"Not excited?"

"As in what? Like did I catch him in the act of masturbation?"

"Shut UP!"

"I wish I could tell you that he put down the phone and started jumping up and down, but he pretty much just set up the appointment."

"Cool."

"If you wanted to analyze his every syllable and pause and breath, you should've made the call, Tate Worm."

"I know," I say. "Shit. That was stupid. Juvenile as all hell. Do you think he thinks it was stupid?"

"I don't think he's thinking about it, is what I think. What I think is you're obsessing."

"I need to get a bathing suit that isn't a bikini," I say. "The kind serious swimmers wear for their journeys across the Irish Channel."

"The Strait of Magellan."

"The Panama Canal."

"The Atlantic," says Kale.

"I draw the line at the Atlantic. That's too far. But will you go with me to get a suit? Tomorrow?"

"I shall. We can go get the stuff at Home Depot for your studio at the same time."

"Excellent thinking, Kale. Did anybody ever tell you you have a fine head on your shoulders?"

"Did anyone ever tell you you are wacko?"

Kale is too beat from her shift to stay up and watch a movie. We turn out the lights and she goes to sleep. She always does—immediately. I lie in my blanket nest on the floor of her room and watch the lights from passing cars stretch up the wall. My thoughts go to Swimmer Boy. I need a cute suit, something sporty but still hot. I think I hear Kale's father snoring. This is familiar—I've been spending nights over here for years. I sleep better in this house. Even before the incident, before the world's fright factor multiplied exponentially, I felt easier here. I only knew I was *un*easy at my own house with my own parents because of the contrast of sleeping at Kale's. These things are intuitive. I just *feel* better, feel safer, and that's how it's always been at the Waggener's. If I could adopt a family, they're it.

Like every night, my thoughts go to my mom and the night it happened. I imagine it. I *see* it. The man's in a mask, almost like Batman's. The back door of my mom's place is unlocked. It's summer. It's light out, for God's sake. It's probably after the run she usually took, and before a late dinner. Had she not just started AA, she would've been having wine or something stronger; that would be a given. But she was a few weeks sober at that point. I have no experience of who she was sober, but still I put her in a chair, with beverage in hand, because she always had a beverage and there's a sound I will always associate with her: ice tinkling in a short, squat glass—glasses you come to learn are for the hard stuff, on the rocks. Maybe it's the same glass and the same ice, but the drink is some mixture of juice and seltzer, or soda water with a twist of lime. Even without the buzz, she likes to tinkle the ice in the glass, nostalgically. She's got the TV on—she was fond of *Wheel of Fortune*—and her feet are up and our cat, Bellboy, is snuggled in her lap. She hears the screen open and shut. *Tate?* she says. (I don't know why I imagine her thinking it was me. I never went over there.) More likely she called out the name of the man she had fallen in love with, the man she was changing her life for. *Kevin,* she might've said. *Is that you?* Maybe she jumped up to go meet him, tossing Bellboy to the floor. Maybe she repeated his name and when he didn't answer, maybe she worried briefly. Or maybe she was so certain it was her beloved that she stayed seated, closed her eyes, arched her neck against the back of the chair, put her lips in the way of a kiss. Maybe Bellboy sensed something—a stranger—a smell he didn't know. Maybe he jumped up, his bell tinkling like the ice, and went to investigate. How much time passed between seeing the face of her killer and the first blow? How much time between then—that pain, the shock— and the blow that knocked her out? What happens when you are dying, the mere moments right after? Do you see tunnels of light like they say? Dead loved ones coming to usher you to the next place? Are those loved ones ready to meet you when it's a murder rather than a prolonged illness? How could they be gathered there with no advance notice? These are the things running through my head as I try to fall asleep. Things I don't share with the therapists, with anyone. Nights are the loneliest time, the darkest. When you are recently dead, and on your way to the next realm, do you dream? If your very brain matter is crushed, do you have memories? Did my mom think of me at the end?

Teenagers can sleep twelve hours a night; it's physiological; we need this much; it's been studied. Kale and I sleep till eleven the next morning. Her parents and little brother are gone when we finally make it downstairs, but they have left blueberry buckwheat pancakes for us—all we have to do is nuke them and add the butter and syrup. Scratch that. *Margarine* and syrup. Butter, Kale reminds me, is an animal product.

"What about the eggs? Doesn't pancake batter have eggs and milk?"

Kale shows me the package—an eggless, dairy-less pancake mix. She shows me the carton of Rice Dream.

"You think of everything," I say. "Is the rest of the family doing the vegan thing just for you?"

"Are you insane?" she says. "Peter?" That's her little brother. "They had normal pancakes, trust me. Or they had something else entirely."

"Your mom made vegan ones just for us? She is the nicest mom on earth."

"She's decent. It's her mission in life to be sure I eat, that we all eat. It's a mom thing."

"My mom never had that thing. I used to have to remind her that people usually eat three times a day, that a normal mother occasionally makes a trip to the grocery store. See, Mom, this is called a grocery cart and look here at all the food one can put in it!"

"You did not say that," Kale says, a big stack of syrupy pancake squares skewered on her fork.

"I know. But practically. I promise you, if I'd become vegan or veggie or anything like that, she would not have made me special meals."

"Agreed."

"You didn't know her all that well."

"True," says Kale. "You and she never spent much time together so I never knew her like you know my mom."

"Priscilla," I say.

"Precisely, Priscilla. You know Pris and John way better than I'll ever know your units."

I finish chewing the over-sized bite I've stuffed into my mouth and wipe syrup from my lips with a paper towel. "That's kinda sad," I say.

"That I didn't know your mom as well as you know mine?"

"No. That the reason you didn't know her is I wasn't spending much time with her."

Kale says it's just the way it is. "Shit happens, Tater Tot."

I make patterns in the syrup with my fork.

"Artie is super cool. I know that." Kale is trying to cheer me up by mentioning my dad, the parent of mine she does know well. She takes her plate to the sink and rinses it before sliding it into the dishwasher rack. "You want OJ?"

"What are the choices?"

"OJ, iced tea, or lemonade." She opens the door of the fridge wider, bends down to look deeper. "Or milk, but you can't have that. Rice Dream."

"I'm not really thirsty," I say. "I just wanted to hear all the bounty Priscilla provided for us."

Kale gives me a look, pours herself a big glass of OJ and drinks it down.

"Race to get ready," she says, and runs for the upstairs shower, leaving me to use the one downstairs.

"Unfair advantage!" I yell after her.

This is the tradition. My clothes are in her room so I have to run up, get them, run down, and by the time I turn on the water, she's probably well into lathering her hair. She beats me every time. When we were younger, it bugged me how Kale always wanted a race, always needed to win. Now, this is just one detail in the whole endearing package that is Kale.

Kale brings the winning suit into the fitting room. I'm striking out with one-piece after one-piece, all of them looking like something you'd wear in the Olympics, or something a grandma would wear to the pool at the local Y. I deplore fitting rooms. Too many mirrors and too much wrong with me. We've been to two stores and the cuter suits are all skimpy and not practical for real swimming, and I'm losing patience with see-ing my half-naked self under ugly lights. Then Kale finds one on the rack outside the fitting room, something someone else rejected. It's the last one of its kind in the store—two pieces, but athletic, a brand that surfers wear. It's a seven, my size, with a chocolate and limey print. Brown is one of my colors—matches my hair and my eyes. The cut makes my arms look buff when they really aren't at all. We move me around in all sorts of ways and it feels very swim-worthy; things stay put. I ask Kale to tell me the truth about how it looks in the back. Cute, she says, it looks cute.

"Do you promise?"

"Tate, I swear. You have a very cute butt. Now can we go? We've still got to pick out paint."

While I'm getting back into my clothes, and getting all these other swimsuits clipped to their hangers, Kale finds flip-flops on sale for six bucks, in the exact limey green of the suit. She holds them up when I emerge. "I'm buying," she says, and gets us both a pair.

At Home Depot we're overwhelmed by color choices. My little studio is all one room with a tiny bath and one of our summer projects is to give it a makeover. Greta is funding the whole thing, to a point, as an early birthday present. She hasn't given me a spending limit, but she said go easy, try to get good deals, and see what you can find at thrift shops. Kale and I found some great vintage stuff, including a lava lamp and an old stereo cabinet that I'm using as a place to put clothes and one of those old chenille bedspreads with the little pom-pom balls on the edges. It's bright yellow.

Kale is laughing at the names of the colors. "Moss," she says to me. "How boring. Whipped Cream. Come on, who are they kidding? This is white."

I look at it. "No it's not; it's definitely more creamy than white."

Kale says, "Oh my God, look how many different versions of white they have!"

I steer her away from the bland. "Come on. We're envisioning something hip and jazzy here."

"How about White Raisin?" Kale holds up a color card.

"Kiwi!" I say, finding a card with that name. "I love kiwi fruit."

"It's like the bathing suit you just bought, that same green."

"It IS!" I say, and we both get the same idea at the same time. We grab for a cocoa-colored card and fight over it. Kale pulls and I pull. Kale twists and the card rips in two.

A sales guy, whose job it is to professionally mix the paints and get you the color you most desire, gives us a look. He assumes we're not actually going to buy anything. People always assume that about kids whose parents aren't present.

"This is the color!" I say to Kale. "With the green!"

"It's perfect. It's called Mountain Bark."

"Mountain Bark'll do."

"Which is the wall color and which is the trim?"

"The brown is the trim. Brown's too dark for the walls."

"We still need something neutral for the ceiling," Kale says. Her dad painted her room last year so she is familiar with all this.

"Greta said the ceiling looks fine like it is—let's just leave it."

"Perfect," says Kale. "Ceilings are a bitch to do anyway—everything drips."

After he mixes each gallon, the sales guy marks the top of the paint can with a smudge of that color, so you know which can is which. Kale, the smart one, remembers to grab two rollers, two brushes, that blue tape that helps keep the trim color from getting on the wall color, and a roller pan.

"Remodel party!" I say, as we take our place in a long line. "We'll order pizza and work all night. Vegan pizza, of course."

Kale says, "I wonder why they don't have a paint color called Ca-Ca. I mean, it's a certain shade of brown we are all familiar with."

"Dude, who would want to paint their bedroom in a color that means shit?"

"I would. I would like to redo my room in a nice shade of boom-boom. Excuse me, sir," she pretends to ask the sales guy, "might you have anything in a bright turd?"

I fold forward with laughter, accidentally hitting the woman in front of me with one dangling can of paint. "Oh! Sorry!"

"Ow!" she says. "Be careful! You girls need to settle *down*."

This sets me off even more. Kale is already running for a different check-out line. When I catch up to her, I say "You are in so much trouble!" and then I bop her on the head with the roller.

Kale calls out, "Assault and battery!" and everyone in the front of the store looks over at us.

"Just kidding," she says to them. "Continue shopping as usual."

We try to hold it together through the self-checkout thing, but when it talks to us, Kale dissolves into hysterics. "All the best to the fam!" she says to the machine, loud enough for everyone to hear. I am out of the store ahead of her, bolting for the car, the laughter so relentless it hurts.

When I arrive at the pool on Tuesday, Sawyer is wearing the same thing he's always wearing. I've got on the new saucy suit with blue jean cut-offs and the matching flip-flops. Sawyer does not comment on my attire. Boys have no clue about such things.

"Hey," I say.

"Hey," he says. "Ready?"

"Ready as I can be at this hour."

"Early for you?"

"Yeah, but it's no problem. You're giving me free lessons. I'll be here at five in the morning if you tell me to."

"That's early, even for me," he says. "I try to schedule my lessons around the trial schedule. But they're in a recess right now, so really I'm wide open if you want to make the next one later."

"Why is there a recess?" I've intentionally not kept up with the trial.

"The judge is in the hospital. Emergency bypass."

"What?"

"He's old. He'll probably be okay, but they had to call a recess till he's back, or else get a new judge to preside. It's messy to switch at this point."

I remind myself to go see Dad after this. So much time on his hands. I'll bring burritos. I'll bring a Butterfinger. I'll stay long enough to play Scrabble.

I stop where Sawyer stops and drop my towel where he drops his, my flip-flops on top. He walks into the water like it's nothing. Sucks in his gut a little, in response to the cold, but keeps on walking. While he's in front of me, I steal glances at his swimmer's body. Suddenly, I just go for it—I dive forward and swim underwater until it numbs me all over. I come up and he's there waiting.

Being this close to Swimmer Boy is taking the blood out of me, making me weak. Or maybe the proximity is pouring blood *into* me. Surging in and out, stomach sinks, chest does the butterfly stroke, brain lacks oxygen. The body contains too much life force or not enough—either scenario an emergency. *Call 911. Someone at Barton Springs needs resuscitating.*

Mouth to mouth.

"Okay," he says. "I'm going to teach you the same way I teach everyone else, but stop me at any point if you feel like we're going too fast or you're tired or whatever." *Not going fast enough* is what I feel.

Sawyer continues: "It's not supposed to be painful—swimming, when you do it correctly, should feel pretty fluid and easy. You take as much advantage as possible of floating."

Take advantage of me is what I think, but what I say is: "Buoyancy. Kale's told me all about it."

"So, the first thing we usually do..."

I interrupt. "Can I just say this friendship is off to a very uneven start? You're teaching me everything—how to swim, how to be a Big, stuff about my dad's trial."

"Well," says Swimmer Boy, "there are things you have more experience with than I do. Like relationships. You and Jasper were like couple of the year or something."

"We were not." I didn't know Sawyer, or remember seeing him, till the day Kale introduced us. I'm surprised to hear he not only knew who I was, but he had an opinion about me and Jasper.

"Well, to me you were. You both seemed, I don't know, wholesome." *Okay, wholesome does not ever equal sexy. He finds me wholesome! I am nine-grain bread.*

"You were good friends," he continues. "I admire couples that start out as friends."

"Kale and Simon are like that," I say. "We all used to play in his treehouse when we were like eight years old. But Jasper and I weren't even together all that long. And he bailed on me, which a friend wouldn't do, because of the whole drama."

"The whole ruined life thing."

"Exactly. He couldn't deal. I mean his parents are *Quakers*. Hello, non-violence."

"Well," Sawyer says. "There are definitely things you could teach me."

My stomach drops out. If only he knew.

"Okay," I say. "We should start before I get hypothermia."

"Right. Today we'll focus mostly on your arms, next time on your kick, and the time after that on your breathing. But we also address everything at once. There's an area of skills we'll emphasize each time, but you need to be weaving it all together eventually."

"Let me warn you—I swim like a total goon."

"I'm sure I've seen worse," says Swimmer Boy.

We do stuff with my arms for a while. We swing our arms wide at the shoulder axis, opening up that joint. *Does he like my surfer girl suit?* He has me imagine that my elbows have puppet strings attached, and a puppeteer is lifting my arm, elbow first, with each stroke. He shakes my arms till they are looser. *Did my boobs just jiggle?* "Let your limbs be rubbery," he says. *All of me is silly putty in your hands.* He continues shaking me out, holding my hands, both at once. Is it my imagination, or does he hold on a little longer than necessary?

On Rule #6, I am so doomed.

CHAPTER TEN:

HER HEAD

Forensics narrows down the murder weapon to something curved, rounded, not sharp. With so many blows to the head, it's hard to isolate the shape of the impact. The average-sized human head is not a lot of surface area for sixteen blows. They overlapped; the skull pretty much deteriorated. Forensics had a challenge on their hands. On *48 Hours* and *Dateline* and sometimes *20/20*, they are often able to tell the exact size and shape of a knife blade, based on the wounds inflicted. They can tell if it's a smooth or a serrated edge. Without even finding any blood on the knife, they can establish the murder weapon. One guy was a chef and a restaurant owner and dumb enough to use an expensive knife that only a professional chef would have. Bingo.

Bludgeonings are harder to decipher. This one has been determined to be done by a curved or rounded edge of something heavy, but not sharp. The edge of a cast-iron skillet has not been ruled out, nor has the rounded backside of a certain type of garden hoe, ostensibly missing from my father's garage.

How in the world do they determine that something is missing from someone's garage? If it's not there, how can you be sure it ever was? The missing hoe...is a hoe some standard item in everyone's garage? Oh my, indeed, where *is* the McCoy family's hoe?

Well, apparently the long wooden handle was found with a bunch of old brooms and mops. Just a long piece of wood, but the end had been sawed off. Based on some identifying marker on the wood, it was determined to be the handle of a certain type of hoe. When I talk to my dad about this, he laughs and calls it "utter nonsense." He never had a hoe, ever, doesn't know what to do with one, has never gardened. Carla was the one who, in good years, filled our yard with blooming things. Dad says he saves wooden dowels like that, broom handles and such, because you never know when you might need one for wedging behind a sliding door when you want to ensure it's locked. Or for dislodging something from a high shelf. *You know me*, he says, *I save things. God only knows why.* He can't remember where the handle in question came from—some old mop or broom or rake—ancient history by now. My father says the homicide detectives in this town are inept. All this time they've spent looking for evidence that doesn't exist while the killer is probably sunning himself in Mexico! The lawyers for the prosecution—utter clowns. They are grasping at straws, he says.

I learn most of what I know about the trial from Sawyer, Swimmer Boy, Reporter Boy. He keeps up with every detail of the case, but never mentions it unless I ask.

We're on our third lesson and buoyancy still escapes me. The more I want to just get it, the harder it is to achieve. Like I want it too badly. Buoyancy, I don't know, it feels almost like a prerequisite for anyone vying for the spot of Swimmer Boy's girlfriend.

He stands waist-deep beside me, holding my head in both of his hands, showing me the way my head would move if I were to do the breathing right, the back and forth, the left and right. "Relax your neck," he says. "Just let it be completely loose." Easier said than done. He is patient, doing the head movement for me, rhythmically, counting it out. *One, two, and left. One, two and right. One, two and breathe. One, two and breathe.* "Feel what it feels like when you're doing it right. Get a sense of that." It feels good—not only the thrill of being close to him, his upper half above the water line a surface I'd like to climb—but the loosening up of my neck, that stalk of tense muscles, the support of the water, the syncopated beat of his voice. I surrender and it starts to feel even better, his sweet hands cradling my skull. "You're getting it," he says. But then I lose it.

"I'm not, don't lie!"

"Tate, you're doing fine. Just relax and stop thinking so hard about everything."

We go at it again. Sawyer turning my head side to side.

I raise my head out of the water and stand up.

"Sorry," I say. "It's the whole head thing. My mother. It's weirding me out."

He takes a second to absorb what I've said. "I can totally see why it would." We just stand there, belly deep in the icy water, people doing whatever they are doing all around us.

"You want to go get ice cream?" he says finally, looking straight at me.

I nod, aware of the muscles it takes to nod, as opposed to the movements my neck has just done over and over, side to side, at the hands of this boy. One who swims. What in God's name does a bludgeoned skull look like? Would it even have a shape? How thick is a skull? How hard to break? My mom and dad and I broke coconuts once in Jamaica, on vacation, when

I was five, and it took a hell of a lot of force to get those things to crack. Is a head like that?

While all those thoughts swim around in my brain, Sawyer never breaks his gaze. He lets me make the next move, which is to say, "Let's go." We're quiet as we walk to the concession stand and wait our turn. The paved walkway is scorching and my flip- flops dangle uselessly from one finger, swinging as I walk. "These actually have a purpose," I say, and I stop long enough to put them on my feet.

So many kids at Barton Springs have learned to swim from Sawyer, he is a celebrity. Shy girls tug frantically on their mother's arms and point toward him. Mothers smile and wave. A boy comes up and gives Sawyer a high five. Swimmer Boy receives all this attention quietly, but keeps his focus on me. At one point when the line is moving and I haven't noticed yet, he touches the small of my back with the palm of his hand, a gentle reminder to move forward. Everything else vanishes at that instant: the mood about my mom, the heat, skulls, the crowds, the kids with their dripping cones. In that instant where he touches me, the unlikely contact of two convex surfaces—a palm, the inward curve of a back, I can't feel anything else.

We are almost to the front of the line before I remember: *No ice cream. I am one inexperienced vegan.* I'm thinking I'll just get lemonade, when the mother in front of us orders Rice Dream. I look up at the board where flavors are listed; for non dairy, there are only three. *Swimmer Boy put his hand on my back!* When the guy asks what we want, I manage to say one scoop, Rice Dream, coconut. I will never be able to stick to my no boys rule.

We take our cones to some trees and sit in the shade.

"If there's anything you want to ask me," he says, "shoot." And even though I can think of a zillion things I want to ask about *him*, I ask him to tell me everything he knows about the murder. Next to the lawyers and the jury, Sawyer is probably the biggest authority on the case. He keeps a fat binder full of notes.

"What do you want to know?" He's all serious, as he should be, as I should be, but all I can do is notice how adorable he is with his shirt back on, with his hair drying a bit in the sun, sitting across from me eating his double scoop of java chip.

My scoop is melting too fast for my mouth to keep up. I perform some managerial licking of drips all around the cone's circumference. *What do I want to know? I want to know what it feels like to kiss you.* In the gap between his question and my answer, thankfully Sawyer can't know all the places my mind travels.

"Her head," I say. "I want to know whatever you know about her head."

CHAPTER ELEVEN:

A Nice Mom and Dad

Maddie's never had Chinese, so I pick something mild for her—a breaded chicken dish that is the closest thing they have to her favorite meal—Chicken McNuggets. While I drive us to Zilker Park, she opens and closes the take-out box, smelling what's inside.

"Mmmm..."

"You like that?" I say. "I think you're going to like it."

Mostly, she seems to like the container, the way the two sides of the top slide into each other to form a lock. Open and close. Open and close. She examines a clear packet of soy sauce.

"Ever had that before?" She shakes her head no.

"Oh, soy sauce is good stuff. It's salty. You like salt?"

Maddie nods.

We park the car and Maddie carries the bag of food while I carry two water bottles and a blanket. We find a flat, grassy spot.

"This looks good," I say. "Here, help me spread this out.

The most fun picnics are on the ground, not on the picnic tables. Those are for families. We're just kids."

I've gotten used to doing most of the talking. Makes sense. At Maddie's age, I probably didn't have a lot to say either. We pull at opposite edges of the quilt to get it just right. "Now," I say, "we take off our shoes to hold down the corners in case it gets windy." I'm wearing my running shoes; Maddie has on those shoes with wheels on the back for tooling around the mall.

"I like your shoes," I say.

"I like your hair," she says.

"Thanks!" It's the first time she's offered something up, not in answer to a direct question. We are making progress, my Little and I. Our first visit was so awkward, I was grateful I'd decided on a movie— two hours during which I didn't have to carry the whole conversation. We shared buttered popcorn and Milk Duds. It was a kids' movie—*Up*—and I hadn't expected to like it much, but it was so good. A couple of parts made me want to cry and if I'd been alone, or with Kale, I would've. But I didn't want to freak Maddie out.

She's finished taking off her shoes and placing them on two corners. Her socks are worn out at the heels; once white, they are now a dingy grey. Maddie and her two younger siblings live with their grandmother. Their mother left shortly after their father got put in prison on drug charges. Maddie's grandmother thinks her daughter-in-law left because she was involved and didn't want to be implicated. Maddie's grandma is a sweet lady who seems too old to suddenly have three little kids. They live in one of the more run-down parts of East Austin.

We eat in silence. Maddie finishes her chicken fast, before I'm done with my veggies and tofu.

"All done?"

She nods.

"I brought a surprise dessert!"

Maddie puts her hand over her mouth like she's already pleased, even though she's not seen what it is yet. I reach into my bag and pull out a foil-wrapped rectangle.

"You like brownies?" There's a nice-sized slab, cut in two.

She nods.

"Well, I hope you like these. They are kind of an experiment, because I had to make them without eggs. I'm trying this new vegan diet. Can't have eggs. I hope they came out okay."

Maddie handles her half carefully, putting her palm under to catch any crumbs while she takes a bite.

"Mmmm..." she says. She smiles and raises her eyebrows.

"I'll take that as a yes."

She looks quizzical.

"You look pleased, so I'll consider that as yes, they came out okay."

Maddie nods and chews.

"I need to go to the bathroom," I tell her. "And it's right over there. Do you want to go with me?"

She shakes her head no.

"Then just wait right here and don't let any ants get my brownie, okay? I'll be right back."

I leave her surrounded by the remnants of our picnic, still chewing. While I'm balanced over the porta-potty, careful not to touch anything, I realize I shouldn't have left her there. Ever heard of abductions, Tate Worm? What kind of a Big am I? Shit.

I have never tried to finish peeing so fast in my life. I almost fall out of the door with my pants still down. Relief: she's sitting right where she was, her back to me.

"I'm back!" I say, and see she is hunched over, quietly crying. There's a little puddle of Chinese food gravy next to one of the empty take-out cartons. Some of it is on her sock. At my arrival, she cries more audibly.

"Honey, what is it?" I put an arm around her.

"I spilled," she says, between intakes of breath.

"Oh, Maddie, that's no big deal. We'll clean it up. It was an accident!" I sit down next to her and give her a side hug. Maddie sniffles.

"Oh, honey. Here." I stand and pick her up. She's short enough and thin enough that her weight feels like nothing. She wraps her legs around my waist and I rub her back as she cries over my shoulder. The gravy on her sock is wet and sticky against my thigh.

When she's stopped crying, she lifts her head but doesn't look me in the eye.

"You feeling better?" I say.

She nods. "Are you going to tell my mom?"

"Absolutely not. One, your mom isn't even around right now, and two, I wouldn't tell her, or your dad or your grandma anything like that. It's not important and it doesn't matter at all." I put her down and have an idea.

"How about you and me go straight to the laundromat and see how fast it is to wash this blanket? And your sock."

"This needed to be washed soon anyway," I say. I have Maddie take her socks off and put her shoes back on sockless. I put my own shoes on, wrap my brownie back up in the foil, and Maddie carries the trash while I carry the bundled up quilt. We dump the bag of trash and walk the rest of the way to the car.

Once we're in the car and she's got her seatbelt on, I turn to her.

"You know what?" I say. "For future reference…I know we only met a week ago, but already I care way more about you than I care about that old quilt."

Maddie looks at her lap.

"In our family, we always relegate the oldest blanket or bedspread or sheet in the house to being the picnic blanket. We *expect* it to get spilled on. We don't even worry about it, because it's just for picnics and sometimes we'll be laying it out on dirt, or on sand at the beach. So it just doesn't have to be pristine."

Why do I keep using words she won't understand? *For future reference, relegate. Pristine* is a word my dad uses that bugs me.

"Picnic blankets are meant for spills is what I mean. So we'll go wash this one, but we don't care if that gravy leaves a stain, because that is what a picnic blanket is for. Okay?"

Maddie nods. "And you're not going to tell?"

"Not going to tell. No reason to. It's not like anything big happened!"

Maddie seems satisfied, so I pull out of the parking lot and head north toward a laundromat in our neighborhood.

I have great memories of going there with my father to wash the blankets and rugs. There was such a clean smell to the place. There was a candy machine right next to the one selling detergent, and once the clothes were in, we'd take some of the change from the roll of quarters and I'd always get a Reese's Cup and Dad always got a Butterfinger. He would tell me if I could guess what he was going to have, he would treat me to whatever I wanted. But 1) neither of us ever veered from those favorite candy bars, so guessing was a moot point; and 2) he was always going to treat. We'd sit by the dryers and eat our candy and Dad would say the candy was our pay for doing this chore, but it never felt like a chore to me.

I think now about how I will let Maddie insert all the quarters and shove the coin receptacle in, a thing I loved to do as a kid. We'll pre-treat the spot, running it under water first, and then applying liquid detergent right to it, rubbing it around. We'll do the same with her one sock, hell with both of them. They could use a trip through a spin cycle.

We're quiet as I drive. I think about turning on the radio, and I wonder which station an eight-year-old girl would listen to, or if she's ever listened. What music does she like? I decide I'm just trying to fill up the silence with noise and I've been learning that silence is okay. Silence is sometimes exactly what everyone needs.

We're stopped at a signal light a few blocks from the laundromat when I finally say something. "You know what I'm thinking of? I'm thinking about how, when I was little, I used to play a game where I pretended that quilt was a magic carpet. You know about magic carpets?" Maddie nods. "Well, I would lay it out in my room and get on, with four of my stuffed animals. I had lots of animals, but for this game I always made myself pick four. That was part of the game—a shortage of space, so I had to be selective. Every time I played, I'd take turns letting different stuffed animals go. And I would pretend we were flying through the air, and I was in charge of my animals' safety way up there. Couldn't let anyone fall off the edge. It was a big job."

Maddie says, "Where was the magic carpet going?"

"Well, that's a good question, because in the game, I don't think we ever arrived at our destination." There I go again, *destination*. "But what I do remember is we were escaping something, my stuffed animals and I. We were sort of running away. The game was about the running more than the arriving."

"Why did you have to run away?"

"Well I didn't really, in real life. It was just a game I liked to play." I pull into the parking lot and stop the car, but Maddie isn't finished asking questions. This is the most she's talked ever.

"Were you running away from a mean mother and father?"

"No. Well, maybe in make-believe. But in real life I have a nice mom and dad." The significance of this assertion hits me hard. *A nice mom and dad*. For a second, I worry I will be the one to cry.

"What other games did you play?" she says.

"Oh, lots of games. You want to play some sometime?" Maddie nods. "We'll do that next time. We'll go to my house and play some games. You know, I didn't have any brothers or sisters so I had to make up lots of creative things to do, with my stuffed animals as the other players."

"The animals were like your brothers and sisters?" she says.

"Yes, pretty much." I figure we will sit here till this line of questioning is resolved, and then I'll usher us into the land of many washing machines, the land where error can be erased, spun out. Maddie is thinking.

"You don't have *any* brothers and sisters?" she says, finally. She makes it sound like I should be in the Guinness Book of World Records for this.

"Nope," I say. "None." I think for a second. "Wait, I take that back."

Maddie looks at me for an explanation. I look right back at her. "I *didn't* have any brothers and sisters," I say. "Now I have you."

CHAPTER TWELVE:

NO CHIMPANZEES

It was Kale's idea to invite Sawyer to our painting party, though I would be lying if I said the thought hadn't crossed my mind. Simon is coming to help, so why not make it the four of us? NOT a double date, I keep telling Kale. I remind her I'm not dating. Having four of us makes it easier to prevent the world of my fantasy, in which Swimmer Boy and I end up swimming all over each other and no actual painting of the walls or trim occurs. I'm starting to think my six month rule was a little harsh; when I wrote down those goals, there was no guy I found even remotely interesting. Then a week later, bam. Enter Swimmer Boy. Still over four months left. Is it possible it's still August? January is two seasons away.

Simon will pick up Sawyer and the pizzas—one without cheese for us vegan heads. Kale and I whip the studio into some kind of shape before they arrive. I was born messy; it is in my genes. I don't know how some people end up neat by nature. It's a huge effort for me to keep the place presentable. My aunts and uncles are prone to dropping in uninvited, unannounced, to see how I'm doing and if I'm keeping up my end of the bargain to not live like a slob. At any point, some-one could decide I belong back in the big house, under closer supervision. At any moment, any behavior of mine (not hanging up my clothes, for example) could be interpreted as psychological instability. One uncle even said as much—that living amidst so much clutter and disorganization was a way I "continue to punish" myself. I didn't even ask him to elaborate on that one. The relatives on Dad's side of the family think healthy people don't have messy living spaces; the relatives on my mom's side are every bit as messy as me. Garbo is possibly worse. Garbo has admitted she has never once wielded a mop, a fact she's slightly ashamed about and has shared with no one but me.

My more persnickety uncle, Jim, is in the big house now, in town to take his turn at attending the trial. Should he drop in tonight, the place will be in decent shape.

Kale brought old sheets from her parents' garage. We move all the furniture to the center of the room, away from the walls, and drape sheets over it all.

"So finish telling me about your Little," Kale says. She is putting blue tape above all the baseboards.

"Well, she was utterly and completely traumatized. She couldn't stop crying."

"About the spill?"

"That's all I could figure. She'd spilled on the blanket and on her sock. It was like she thought she was going to be *beaten* or something." I pull off another long strip of tape and Kale applies it low on the wall. "You're good at this, Leafy Green."

"Experience," she says, "is the mother of invention."

"I thought curiosity was."

"No," she says. "Curiosity killed the cat." Weirdly, Bellboy jumps into my thoughts. I imagine his exact weight in my arms, the feel of his fur next to my face. I wish we knew if he was alive. It wouldn't have made sense for the killer to kill him, too. Not like he could talk about what he'd seen.

"Necessity!" I say. "Necessity is the mother of invention. That's it. You need something, you make something. You invent."

"It's more fun though if you mix them up," says Kale.

"The rolling stone," I say, "gathers no…artichokes!" I use my best orator's voice.

"Good one. Nor moss, among other things it could gather."

"Nor cans of paint. Nor friends," I say. This overuse of the word 'nor' reminds me of Bower.

"The rolling stone gathers no chimpanzees," says Kale.

"Chimps! I couldn't agree with you more!" I get her a chair to stand on for taping off the top of the door frame. "What the hell does that saying mean, anyway? The rolling stone gathers no moss. Who comes up with these things and who decided they were worth repeating for all time?"

Kale says, "I think it's about planting roots. If you move around all the time, as the rolling stone does, you never get a chance to accumulate anything permanent. Moss is the permanence—it can only grow on something still, right?" she says. "I don't know. Something like that. That's weird though, about Maddie flipping out."

"It was heartbreaking. She was inconsolable. Kept asking me if I was going to tell."

"Yikes. Someone in her life over-reacts to simple spills."

"Someone hits the kids to the point of abuse."

"That sucks," says Kale. "It's a very good thing she has you in her life."

We see the headlights from Simon's car and we hear the car doors slam.

"Do I look goofy in this?" I say, examining again what I've chosen to wear—overall shorts with a tank top underneath.

"You look smashing. You look precisely appropriate for someone who's going to spend the night getting messy with paint."

"Hey!" I say when I open the door. I think I say it a little too fast. Sawyer has on professional painter pants that have already been christened with multi-colored splotches. "Look at you." Sawyer sort of sashays around me into the small space. Kale takes the pizza boxes and kisses Simon hello. Simon puts a bag of something on the kitchenette counter.

"Hey Tate," he says. "Can I put these brewskies in the fridge?"

"Sure," I say, just as Kale says, "Beer?"

Kale is anti-drinking, for different reasons than I am. Her reasons have nothing to do with growing up with an alcoholic mom; she's just a health freak and it's been proven alcohol kills brain cells. She wants to keep all her brain cells. Kale likes being smart.

Simon offers us each a beer.

"Who bought it for you?" Kale asks. "You're not exactly twenty-one."

"I bought it. The guy at the convenience store near the airport—the one who works weekends—he doesn't card anyone."

Sawyer passes on the beer, waving it off with one word: "Swimming." He's a competitive swimmer. He needs to be in good shape.

I also turn down Simon's offer, saying, "Did you know one out of four children of alcoholics will become alcoholics?" Then I feel like a dork, spouting off statistics. "As an only child, where does that leave me? One out of four—I'm the only one!" I laugh. I try to turn this funny.

Simon takes a swig of his beer—*Corona*—which if I was going to like beer, might be a brand I'd choose. I like the tall, clear, long-necked bottles, and the way at restaurants they serve them with a wedge of lime. "Not like I'm going to drink the whole six-pack. I was bringing it for all of us. It goes good with pizza."

"I'm starving," I say, grabbing paper plates from the cabinet. I offer people water or limeade. We sit on the floor since all the furniture is displaced. Kale and Simon are against the wall; Sawyer and I sit cross-legged, less than an inch between his knee and mine.

"You live here by yourself?" Sawyer asks.

"Well, yes, but someone from my dad's or mom's family is always in the big house. They keep an eye on me, which gets very old. Everyone is waiting for me to fall apart."

Sawyer has his mouth full. He nods. Simon is also busy eating. Kale is taking individual mushrooms off her slice of cheese-less pie and dropping them into her mouth. I give her a look that says, *oh my God, one who swims is in my studio! Do something! Say something!* At a loss, Kale says, "Good pizza," and gives me the look right back.

Simon says, "I feel sorry for you two. What is pizza without the melted cheese?"

Sawyer laughs. "My dad is lactose intolerant," he says. "So I'm used to seeing pizzas like that."

"What does your dad do?" Kale asks.

"Don't you remember?" I say. "One-who-saws—he's a carpenter."

"Cabinetmaker, really. He can build houses and stuff, but mostly he makes custom furniture."

"That's probably why you just so happened to have painter pants with paint already on them," I say.

"Yup," Sawyer says. "When he does work on houses, he makes me help."

"My cousin makes good money painting houses on the New Jersey shore," Simon says. "Last summer I went and helped. Saved money."

"Houses in beach communities need to be painted really often," Sawyer says. *Beach communities!* He's adorably nerdy. He's the boy who knows everything. "Salt air," he adds.

Kale raises her eyebrows at me—a look that echoes what I just thought: *Listen to Swimmer Boy reeling off the facts!*

Everybody engages with their pizza for several minutes and I remind myself silence is okay. Simon finishes his beer and burps.

"Nice one," says Kale.

"You're welcome," says Simon. They are like an old married couple, those two.

I take another slice and try to think of something to say. It's harder with more of us here. At Barton Springs, Sawyer and I never run out of things to talk about.

Simon gets up for another Corona. The mini-refrigerator hums. He puts the empty bottle in the recycling crate and it clatters against the plastic. Every sound is exaggerated because no one is talking. I jump up to put some music on. I mean, duh. Finally Kale says, "Tater Chip here was just contemplating the origins of the expression, 'the rolling stone gathers no moss.'"

I almost spit out my mouthful of limeade. "Excuse me? That was you. That was Leafy Green who was pondering that."

"And what did she come up with?" Sawyer says, smiling.

"Well, she didn't speculate on the origins exactly, but she interpreted the meaning," I say. "Kale thinks it's about permanence—and how people who move around too much can't really plant roots or accumulate anything."

"Mostly," Kale says, "we were having fun filling in the blank with different words, like 'the rolling stone gathers no artichokes' was one of Tate's. A fine adage, don't you think?"

"Chock full of wisdom," says Sawyer.

"Exactly," I say. "And there are endless possibilities for what the stone can't gather."

"Rolling stone gathers no paint rollers," Simon says. "No beer." He raises his bottle in a toast.

I raise my glass of limeade. "The rolling stone gathers no cheeseless pizza."

"No tampons!" Kale says.

"No condoms!" Simon says.

"Ewww," Kale says. "The rolling stone gathers no dog dookie!"

"Dookie!" I say, because this is a new one.

Sawyer's the only one not contributing.

Kale says, "Swimmer Boy?"

Sawyer takes a sip of his water. "The rolling stone," he says, "gathers no...buoyancy."

"Priceless," says Kale. "Buoyancy. I think buoyancy is the winner. Makes me want to go swimming! Should we?"

"We're supposed to paint," I say. I'm so left out of this whole buoyancy experience.

"Ah yes," says Kale. "Alas, Tate Worm brings me back to reality."

"Besides, buoyancy is over-rated," I say. "Buoyancy isn't all it's cracked up to be."

"You've never felt it yet," Kale says.

"Exactly. In all the times I've flailed about in the icy springs of Barton, I've never found my buoyancy. And maybe I never will, so maybe we should stop talking about it. It's like this club I'm not a member of."

The door opens, and Uncle Jim barges in. We all look at him.

"How's it going?" he says.

"Ever heard of knocking?" I say.

"Sorry, honey," he says, and then, "Who bought the beer?"

Nobody says anything. I get up and hand him the remainder of the six-pack. "Here," I say. "All yours. Enjoy."

Simon is caught red-handed, the only one with a beer on the floor in front of him.

"Is someone going to tell me where you got the beers?" Jim says.

Simon says, "I brought them. No big deal. I just like beer with pizza."

"Your parents know you drink beer?"

Simon shrugs. "I'm not sure."

The lecture ensues. We are going through a serious legal battle right now, one where my father's entire future is on the line. This is no time to be disregarding the law—we are all underage and if anyone were to see this, it would be another strike against my father, against the whole family. What is wrong with us that we can't see this? That we would take such a risk at a time like this? He's surprised at us, and he's mostly surprised at me. He would think I would exhibit better judgment. He hates to say it, but this is the kind of thing that will cause me to lose my privilege of living in the studio. He's going to have to talk it over with my dad. I glance at Kale, then Sawyer. I'm embarrassed he's witnessing this display, this *avuncular* display. Avuncular was one of Bower's vocabulary words. It means "pertinent to an uncle" and I am not lying. I could not even make up something that weird.

"Are you finished?" I ask. "Because we want to paint the room now—we've got it all ready."

Kale chimes in. "I can totally see your point, Uncle Jim. This was stupid on our part. Nobody here is a drinker. Nobody is drunk. But it was a dumb risk to take. We apologize."

Kale is always perfect in these moments. Makes us all look shiny.

"For the record," I add. "I don't drink. For the obvious reason that my mother was an alcoholic. I have zero interest in being like her."

"Point taken," says Uncle Jim. He is so serious, so straight-laced, so opposite of *fun*. Compared to him, my dad is a carnival.

Jim says good night and tells us to wrap this party up before midnight. When he's out the door, I make a face.

"God," I say. "It's like I have six parents now. Whoever thinks I am without parents, let this be known: they are multitudinous."

"Good word," says Kale. I want to remind her about avuncular, which will make her laugh, but she's turned to Simon. "Nice going," she says. She pretends to beat him up, then kisses him. I look anywhere but at Sawyer while they smooch.

Simon, as if doing penance, gathers up all the dinner trash and throws the pizza boxes into the outside garbage can. I lower the music and wipe up the crumbs and grease spots on the counter. Uncle Jim left us all in a bleak mood, but at least we are off the subject of buoyancy.

Kale decides we should have a race and get this puppy painted in no time. She and Simon will do one side of the studio and I'll be teamed up with Swimmer Boy on the other side. He takes trim and I take walls and Kale says, "Ready, set, GO."

CHAPTER THIRTEEN:

FORGETTING

Apparently, there is a God.

We're at Barton Springs for my last lesson when Sawyer tells me the latest news about the trial. An anonymous tip has been sent to the lawyers for the defense, stating that the person who killed Carla McCoy was not her husband Arthur, but an unnamed man she dated briefly, someone she met online. The anonymous informant made the call from a pay phone.

"How'd the guy know all this?" I ask Sawyer.

"The informant? He claims someone told him about it in jail. Some guy who knew the killer said something and then the guy he told it to, the informant, was released—charges were dropped on whatever he was in for. He'd known your dad in jail, and liked him. He felt he had to tell someone what he knew. So he made the anonymous call."

"But now he's not anonymous, right?" I ask. "They know who he is."

"They will. Just a matter of time. They just have to narrow it down. Either they'll find him or he'll come forward. He'll be a key witness."

Sawyer reads my mind, opens his arms for a hug, and I fall into it.

"God," I say. It feels like a hug I belong to. Like a club. Or family.

"I know," he says. He squeezes me tighter. I feel him smell my hair and I'm glad I just washed it.

"God," I repeat. "This is such a huge relief." And I mean both things—my dad's innocence confirmed, of course. But it's also a relief to finally be body-to-body with Sawyer. Since we're both in swim suits, there's not a lot between us. With school about to start, I would be sad about this last lesson, but fortunately the end of lessons doesn't mean the end of our time together. In the last week, we've talked on the phone every day. Kale says it's just a matter of time before I bail on Goal #6. But for now, we are just friends. Tell that to anyone walking by us right now. We can't seem to stop this hug.

Sawyer pulls back first, just far enough to look at me. "Hey," he says.

"Hey," I say. I look down. "Thanks for telling me."

"I'm very happy for you and your dad," he says.

"And," he adds, "at this moment I'm also very happy for me."

I look at him, acknowledge with my eyes that what he's just said constitutes flirting. "Yeah? Well I'm happy for both of us."

Hard as it is to break the hug, I do. "So, what do you want me to do today?" I'm pulling my hair into a ponytail, which is the closest I've come to wearing a swim cap. Too goofy. I don't mind the goggles, which are around my neck.

"You ready to just swim, long distance?"

"I'm ready to try."

"Let's start in the shallow end with some stretching and get used to the temperature. Then we'll send you off to tackle your first mile."

"I can't do a *mile*."

"Don't think of it as a mile, just think stroke by stroke, think about finding your center and the point where you are buoyed by the water."

"Roger that, Swimmer Boy…heretofore referred to as my buoyancy."

"You crack me up," he says. "The things you say. Heretofore. You sound like the lawyers."

"Objection!" I say. "Over-ruled!"

Sawyer says, "Badgering the witness!"

We're in the shallow end, immersed from the knees down. No matter how many times I go to Barton Springs, the temperature is always a shock. The first full immersion, painful. I hate anticipating it, so I go ahead and dunk myself, wanting to get that first jolt over with. Sawyer does the same, but doesn't act like it's any big deal.

"Damn," I say, coming up. "This must be what it feels like to be in the morgue." And then I want to kick myself for always saying inappropriate, death-related things. I tell myself to shut *up*.

"Ready to do your first mile?"

"Wait. Review with me again what I'm supposed to do?"

"Just swim, find the place where your body floats just below the surface of the water, the place where it takes the least effort to stay up. That's the place where you'll be able to just go and go and go. But you have to relax into it. Trust it. Then just keep doing what you've done every time, what you've practiced doing with your arms, your kick, your breathing side to side. Do it till you forget you're doing it," he says.

"Easy for you to say."

I put my goggles on and check the seal, wedging them into my eye sockets. I say "Here goes nothing," and then I push off from the bottom and head toward the far end. Five laps constitute a mile, but I can't think about that. Instead I do what Sawyer said, and think about each stroke following the one before it, about finding a place where the water wants to cradle me, where it's more like rest than work.

At first, I'm totally focused on counting, on breathing, on checking that I'm using all the strategies Sawyer has taught me. I envision the puppeteer lifting each arm by the elbow, which, when it works, makes the arm part feel fluid and effortless. I remind myself to *slow down*, this is not a race. This is about endurance. I find a pace I think I can sustain for an hour or however long this mile is going to take.

A game show buzzer goes off in my head: Foul! Penalty! Do not think about the *mile*, just keep swimming. I'm aware that it's not nearly as hard as it once was, and I've got the breathing thing down. The only time I falter is when I collide with another swimmer. I stop, tread water for a sec, and then put my head back in the water. Proceed.

Too fast. Go slower. Not a race. Find the place where the body floats.

At some point, I stop thinking about the doing of it, and I'm just doing it, which frees up my mind to think about my dad. This new anonymous tip in his favor. How soon could he get out? How obvious will it be to the jury that he's innocent? Surely this new piece of evidence will be enough to create reasonable doubt in their minds. I think about the studio, how I love the colors, how much I would like to invite Sawyer over some night when Kale and Simon aren't there. I feel lucky: what other girl who's on the brink of seventeen has a place of her own where she could have a dreamy boy over? I look up to see I'm moments from having to turn around—one fifth of the way through and not tired. Not gasping. Not flailing. I think about Jasper, how thoroughly he dropped me, how even before he did that, he started acting like he didn't care. He'd been crazy about me, insatiable on all matters Tate, and then, without warning, he was looking for reasons we couldn't spend time together. I get it. He didn't want to stay with a girl whose family situation made national news. *Excuse me!* Bumper cars with another lap swimmer. A lady. We smile and get back on our respective tracks. I wonder if Sawyer's able to see me, how I'm acing it so far, this first mile of mine as a new fish. Funny, I'm not cold anymore. What I feel, temperature-wise, is this perfect combo of sun on my back, a radiant warmth, and coolness from below. The two temps meet somewhere inside me and balance each other out. Water is miraculous when you think about it. *Water*. Matter you can move through, matter you can ingest, utilize, then pee out. Matter that can carry you. Lettuce: 95% water. The human body: 50 to 65% water. Planet Earth: a full 71% water. There's huge amounts of it under the ground; this very spring, part of a whole underground system called the Edwards Aquifer. I'm headed back the other way, on the third of five laps now, without even remembering doing the turn-around. *Forgetting. Forgetting I am swimming.* I think of Swimmer Boy, who must be doing something now to kill time while I prove myself. *Killing time.* Strange expression. My dad must be very acquainted with what it is to kill time. He has had to kill a lot of it. Time is perhaps something he's capable of killing. Why do they choose the word *kill*, when really they just mean *passing* time? Why must it be killed, offed, made to no longer exist, violent-prone? Like accident-prone. Like Carla. Never without a bruise or a sprain or a burn. A bandage, a scrape, a puncture, a gash. *How'd you do that?* The little glass candle holder exploded when she picked it up—hot wax all over her wrist. She sprained an ankle by jumping funny into some guy's pool. Or she couldn't remember. She'd say she bumps into things too often to recall which bump led to which bruise. It was the drinking, of course, but as a kid I didn't know that. Usually kids are the ones with skinned knees, with Band-Aids. *Carla. Mom. Mom, Carla. Dead. Like time.*

Being dead might be like swimming, if we're lucky. An existence in a watery place where we're not our human form anymore, but something with gills, something formless even, buoyant, afloat, able to be everywhere at once. Able to leap continents in a single bound. Ocean to sea. Aquifer to spring. Being dead might just be the smallest detectable essence of existence. Maybe Carla is, in the afterlife, finally finding her buoyancy. Wouldn't it be nice if being dead were similar to before we are born? Warm and wet and dark, afloat in a sea of amniotic fluid.

Sawyer. Swimmer Boy. Where is he? I most definitely swam to the point of forgetting. I've most definitely found my buoyant spot just below the surface of the water here at Barton Springs. Is he seeing? Does he know? Which lap am I on? Which way am I headed? Where's Mom? Can she see me from where she is? Jasper, all those Finches, who needs them? Uncle Jim and his warning lectures. My studio, all chocolaty and key lime pie. I need a cool couch, something retro, something like would've been on that old show *The Jetsons.* A family who lived in the outer space of the future. I've lost count now. Lost time. No, killed it. Someone might see me and think, *Swimmer girl.* Think, *Boy that girl can swim!* Someone might think it's hard, doing this, but they just don't know yet about buoyancy, and then it hits me that I now know, what Kale and Sawyer have been talking about all this time. I know it. I'm feeling it. I'm *in* it. I could swim forever. I'm almost seventeen. I'm a vegan, big sistering, boyfriend-avoiding girl—one who swims.

I bump into someone and look up and it's Sawyer.

"Hey," he says. "You ever going to stop?" and I say something back, in a fish language. I say something from my gills, in and out, watery words that aim to tell him where I've been, but fail.

"You did six," he says.

"What?"

"Laps. You swam *six* already. You did it. You more than did it!"

I take off my goggles and let them drop like a necklace against my chest. I'm not cold. I'm not tired. I'm energized. I could just keep going. I could swim to China. I hear Kale's voice: *The Strait of Magellan. The Atlantic.*

What I say to Sawyer is none of this. "Cool," is what I say.

"You kidding?" he says, "This is more than cool. You were amazing. You were Swimmer Girl!"

And I want to tell him how I know that, how I felt it, how unmistakable it was once I arrived there, at my buoyancy, how I've been thinking of everything imaginable this last hour or whatever it's been, this timeless time, this bit of time not killed but enlivened. This slice of time completely revived, hydrated. "I felt that," I say. "It was easy. I forgot I was doing it, like you said I would."

Sawyer hugs me and our skin is cold, pickled. He kisses the top of my wet head.

Swimmer Boy just kissed me. Not that the head is the sexiest place to receive a first kiss, but it's sweet. Like something a parent might do to a child. Something a Big might do to a Little. Something so innocent, it doesn't encroach on any of my vows.

"Let's celebrate," he says. "This and the news about your dad."

"Okay. What should we do?"

Sawyer says, "I have an idea. Leave it to me. And by the way, congratulations on your graduation from Sawyer Madison's Swim Academy. We need to get you a cap and gown."

"A swim cap!"

"Perfect. And the gown can be a towel."

"Toga-like."

We are walking up the bank toward the snack bar, when I see Jasper Finch and his buddies, looking straight at me. At *us*. At me with Swimmer Boy. We are holding hands, we are talking and laughing and joking; one might describe us as *jubilant*. Jasper gives a weak, forced smile. His friend to the left pokes him. Sawyer loosens his grasp on my hand, but I reassure him by tightening mine on his.

"Hey there," I say.

Jasper says, "Tate."

Sawyer holds out the hand that isn't holding mine, and says his name, by way of introduction. I chide myself for not being the one to do that, to say, hey, this is Sawyer, reporter boy, one who swims, *my new beau in the making*.

"Nice to meet you," says Jasper. Then, to me, "Hey, I was glad to hear that good news about the trial."

Wow. Word travels fast.

"Yeah," I say. "Me too. Well, see ya." Jasper looks kind of lost, kind of shocked. Jasper looks a lot like how I must've looked the day he broke up with me. Like he's just been spun off an amusement park ride, and landed hard, right on his heart.

As we get out of their range of hearing, I say, "AWK-ward!"

"Definitely awkward," Sawyer says. "I feel sorry for him."

"Do not feel sorry for him. He is the one who broke up with me and he had no trouble at all doing it."

"I feel sorry for him now, not then," Sawyer says. "He's probably realizing now just how much he gave up."

I look at Sawyer, whose hand I'm most definitely holding. "You're sweet," I say. "You are like the sweetest boy that ever lived."

Sawyer just smiles, and we are on our way, chugging up

the hill, ex-boyfriend behind me, finally really behind me. We are headed off to whatever celebration Sawyer has in mind. *Leave it to me,* he said. I like a guy who has ideas.

CHAPTER FOURTEEN:

CHIVALRY

Pedernales Falls is where he takes me and it is the perfect place. I've been before, but only twice, once with my father when I was small, and once with Kale and Simon. The rocks Sawyer and I sit on are huge and pale and marble-smooth. The water squeezing through the rock channels is loud and frantic. If you sit close to the falls, you have to yell to hear each other. In his backpack, Sawyer has the closest thing we can get to champagne—sparkling apple cider. He puts down the pad he sleeps on when camping and unloads a baguette, a ripe avocado, a jar of gourmet mustard and another jar of tapenade. He's got *vegan brownies*. He procured all this after dropping me at home to shower and change.

"It's like someone told you my favorite foods!" I say.

"Maybe someone did."

"Who? Kale?"

"Maybe I'm psychic," he says. "Maybe I can read you."

"Well, tapenade is one of my favorite things ever. In New Orleans, where my Aunt Greta lives, they have these warm sandwiches called muffalettas, and they have a chopped olive spread on the French bread. They are so yummy. I'm a huge fan of olives!"

I take a hunk of bread and spread it with the tapenade and take a bite.

"I can't believe you thought of everything—a little knife, and napkins. Cups for our bit of the bubbly! Somebody trained you well."

"My mom. She can put together a great picnic. For any occasion."

"Yeah?" I say. "I'd like to meet your mom. She did a good job with you."

"My mom cooks gourmet meals, even when we're camping. Over a camp stove. Things like crawfish etouffee and stuffed portabella mushrooms."

"Wow."

"She loves a challenge. Once, she even made egg rolls on a camping trip. And crepes—she regularly makes crepes. She says people who think you have to use that freeze-dried crap just because you're camping are nuts. I mean, sure, if you're wilderness backpacking and have no way to keep things cold—then you're limited somewhat. But if you're car camping and have a cooler? Sky's the limit for her."

Right then, in the middle of eating my baguette smothered with tapenade, I start crying. Sawyer doesn't notice at first, keeps on talking about all the amazing things his mom has made on camp stoves. Gumbo. Blackberry cobbler. I wipe my eyes on my napkin, blow my nose.

"Hey," he says. "What happened?" The sound of my nose-blowing strikes me as comical and I laugh. He scoots over closer to me and encircles me with his arm. I'm crying again. He looks at my face, trying to discern my mood. I'm like that tragedy/comedy mask that often accompanies theatrical productions.

"Look at me; I'm ridiculous!" I'm making myself laugh.

"Just tell me what it is."

"You talking about your mom. One, I want memories like that; and two, I want my mom back." That does it. I'm balling again. I'm a friggin' waterfall of sadness and regret. I'm one big motherless aquifer of tears.

Sawyer holds me and holds me and holds me—he's my buoyancy—and I cry it all out. We sit like that for I don't know how long, some amount of time killed, there by the falls. The bread getting hard and sharp where it was last broken off, the avocado going from green to brown, the bubbles in the sparkling cider ceasing to sparkle.

When I finally speak, I say, "I'm sorry. I ruined our picnic." I'm reminded of Maddie, how she came unglued.

Sawyer grabs a hard hunk of bread and spreads it with smooth avocado. "Who says it's ruined?" he says.

"Don't break your teeth," I say, smiling. He bites it, and makes a face like he's chewing on glass.

I punch him in the shoulder, the same one I've been crying on. "You're wet," I say.

Sawyer says, "Swimmer Boy likes being wet. If he's not wet, he'll dry up and disintegrate."

"You know what?" I say.

Sawyer says the requisite *what*?

"I want to kiss you so bad right now I could die."

Sawyer says he is open for business. He would hate for me to die over something so attainable as this.

"I haven't told you yet about my stupid goal."

"Goal?"

"This goal says I will not be with a guy romantically for six months."

Sawyer whistles. "From now?"

"No. From when I made the goal, which was in early July.

Maybe late June. I don't know. No, I'm lying. It was July, fair and square. January is when it's over."

"That blows," he says. I find this funny because I've never heard Sawyer say anything even close to a swear word.

"It does. It blows big-time."

"It *sucks*."

"It absolutely does suck the largest weenie ever." My saying the word *weenie* makes him laugh.

"Who made the goal?"

"I did, thank you very much."

"Well, if you made it and if you now think it's stupid, then you could stop it," he says.

"I'll ponder that and get back to you. It made a lot of sense at the time. And it probably still makes sense. It's just harder now that there's you."

Sawyer stretches the piece of plastic wrap the brownies came in, pulls it with both hands, watches it get wavy and rippled before it gives. Like those heat waves in the Grand Canyon.

"Must you torture the plastic wrap?" I say.

"There you go again," he says, "saying hysterical things."

"We're still buds?"

"I hope we're more than that. You forget I teach children. If I've learned anything, it's patience. I can wait till January if you can. I'm not going anywhere."

"I'm afraid you could sweep me off my feet, Sawyer Madison. In January, that is."

Sawyer fills up our plastic glasses with the now non-sparkly beverage—first mine, then his. "We forgot to do a toast," he says.

"To buoyancy!" I shout.

"To your success in the pool today...*and*..." He holds the glass higher still. Pedernales Falls tumbles behind us.

"And to picnics, and to my dad!"

"And to the quickest fall in history," he says.

"Yes!" I say. "Most definitely! May autumn *fly*."

Plastic glasses click. We drink.

I pick up his hand and kiss the back of it, like a knight would do to a lady.

I say, "Who says chivalry is dead?" and Sawyer is laughing again.

CHAPTER FIFTEEN:

WHO I AM

On *Dateline*, which is my reward for finishing my homework, there's a story of a man who is shot and killed while in bed with his wife. His kids and step-daughter and her friend are sleeping down the hall. In an interview, his wife says she didn't see the shooter. She was woken by the gunshot, saw her husband had been shot ("I will never get that image out of my mind!") and saw a shadow of a person leaving their bedroom. They keep asking her: "You didn't see who it was? You only saw a shadow?" A shadow, the woman repeats. (This is her story and she's sticking to it!) After a commercial break, things get really skanky. First, the woman reveals that she and her husband were "swingers." They met up with other people—couples and singles—who wanted to be sexually adventurous. They would swap partners. The woman acted like this was the grandest thing. She said unlike when your husband has an affair, there's no lying, no betrayal. (*Right*, I'm thinking. *Still sounds pretty terrible to me.*) They go along their married lives for a time, swinging on the weekends, until the wife sleeps with a man she falls for, and begins to want to be with *him* for eternity. (Enter the gun. The shadow!) She claims she was in love with her husband and only having fun with the other man; she claims she would never have wanted her husband dead. The reporters for *Dateline* get waylaid on a tangent about this huge collection of pornography they found in the couple's bedroom. (Hello? Their sexual deviance has already been established.) They show some pictures of magazines splayed out like a bad poker hand. They have to drag it out to be an hour-long show, so they talk about the kids who were in the house, they show photos—the kind that get taken every fall at every school in the world. Missing front teeth, bad haircuts, forced and crooked grins. Finally, after an unusually long station break, the truth comes out! The friend of the step-daughter cannot stop having nightmares about what she saw. She comes forth to tell that her friend killed the step-dad, because she knew her mom wanted him out of the picture. As a minor, the daughter thought she could do the killing and save her mom the whole life-in-prison thing. (Again, I am bamboozled. Even this swinger woman can't figure out that the way to go would be simple divorce?)

School started and mostly it's boring. No classes with Sawyer. Kale and I chose creative writing with Bower, because we want to grow up to be as knowledgeable about language and literature as she is.

She does vocabulary once a week, and she organizes the lesson around Latin roots. So for example, one lesson used the suffix *–cide,* which means "the killing of." She put a whole list of words on the board: suicide (killing of self), patricide (killing of father), matricide (killing of mother), genocide (to kill off a whole people), sororicide and fratricide (sisters and brothers, like sororities and fraternities). There was even one called infanticide—unthinkable!

Killing of a mother is pretty unthinkable, too.

Sawyer has to take the journalism English class option. So that blew our chances of getting a class together. We didn't even get the same lunch period. It blows. It blows a giant saxophone.

It's important, during long boring spells of nothing but school, to remember what one has to look forward to. My chronological list: every two weeks, an outing with Maddie; soon, my birthday; and then Christmas; and somewhere in there, my dad getting released—you'd think it would be soon now that another man is known to be responsible, but the legal machine is a slow-running one, a machine in desperate need of a tune-up, new spark plugs. It could be months, who knows. I look forward to January, and that one's obvious.

But till then, *Dateline* helps get me through because 1) I see situations worse than my own, and this makes me feel better; 2) I see situations pretty similar to my own, and this makes me feel I have company in the world of family drama; and 3) I see situations where after a lot of ruckus and heartbreak, innocent people are freed. It's only a matter of time for my dad. I look forward to having at least one biological parent again.

Lately, the episodes that interest me more are the ones about people my age, not married people, but young people who do horrible things or extraordinary things, like a girl who nearly escapes her abduction by making all sorts of noise from the trunk of the car, or the two girls who fight over one guy, and eventually get so caught up in it that one of the girls stabs the other one. *Kills* her. They're in high school. They call this episode "Deadly Rivalry." These shows take the emphasis off fathers murdering mothers and make me feel better about who I am—were I not the daughter of a murdered woman, I would never in a million years end up doing something worthy of getting me on one of these dismal shows. I'm not extraordinary. And not one to stab another girl over a boy. Seriously. I'm about as normal as they come.

That is, if someone who watches these shows as religiously as I do can be called normal. Sawyer has asked if he can come watch with me sometime, but watching is something I like to do in private. And that's probably weird, too.

CHAPTER SIXTEEN:

GOLDEN

My mom used to tell people that I was a fall baby. I remember thinking that meant a baby who fell down a lot. Carla explained it to me—fall as in autumn. She said I'd been born during a colorful month—the red, gold, green and brown of changing leaves, the bold orange of pumpkins, round and ripe and ready for their jack-o-lantern futures. October 17th.

We moved from Illinois before I turned three, so I don't remember what fall was like there. Here in Austin, mid-October is still pretty warm. The only thing that differentiates the time around my birthday from summer is school. By that time, I feel entrenched in the new school year. The first report cards have come out. I make good grades without a lot of effort, so the concurrence of report cards and my special day never puts me at risk for having a bad birthday or getting my party revoked, which happened to Simon once.

This day, though, is supposed to be different. This year it's the Golden Birthday. Seventeen on the seventeenth. Whoop-de-doo. Kale tried to get me to plan something really snazzy— to combine the unveiling of the newly painted studio with a birthday bash and have a bunch of people over. Like who? It's not like we have dozens of friends. Her thought was fancy appetizers with fizzy drinks in real wine glasses. Fill up the studio with teenagers. *Invite your Uncle Jim*, she said. *Wouldn't want anyone to have too much fun!* But I wasn't in the mood to plan a party for myself, given all the reasons I have to *not* celebrate. I mean, how would it feel for my dad to know his only child is turning seventeen, throwing an adult kind of party, her first one, and he can't even come and hold up a glass and say cheers? And what about the parents of the people I'd invite? How many of them would want their kids coming over to this house, where you could stage the next episode of *Dateline*? To be honest, putting myself in the place of such parents, I don't think I'd want my kid to go. Who's supervising? *The brother of the prime suspect. The sister of the deceased.* Something about those McCoys just isn't right.

Greta also tried to talk me into something—a weekend away with her. She said for her, seventeen was a big one. A hell of a lot happened in the year between seventeen and eighteen. "If you recall," I tell her, "a hell of a lot has already happened to me." Garbo can't argue with that, but she says there are happenings and there are happenings. That stuff happened *to* me. The stuff she is referring to might be things that I have more say in, things that I let happen, or make happen. In the end, we settle on just having Greta come to town, but no trip, no big plans. I tell her we can see a matinee or something. I can beat her butt at miniature golf.

That morning there are three voicemails lined up on my cell. First, from Dad. "Happy day, sweetheart. I wanted to be the first to say it. You're no doubt still sleeping, but I hope it's a fantastic birthday. Bye-bye." Next, Garbo: "Wake up and smell the birthday coffee, birthday girl! So, my flight's going to be a half-hour late. Don't forget to come get me so we can party hardy." And the third one is Sawyer: "Hey Tate. Happy birthday! Call me if you want to do something." Sawyer knows I'm keeping this birthday mellow, and unlike Kale and Greta, he doesn't try to change my mind.

He's the one I call back right away.

"Hey," I say. "You want to go with me to get Garbo from the airport later?"

Sawyer stumbles around his words. He does want to, but he can't. His dad is making him help with some construction project till later.

"One who saws needs help from one who swims?" I say. "What are they building? A waterpark?"

"Ha."

Sawyer agrees to call later and stop by. He has something for me.

I spend the rest of the morning doing laundry, taking a shower, finding something to wear, and straightening up the studio. Greta hasn't seen it since all the changes, most of which she funded. I take the two throw rugs outside and shake them. Given the amount of dust that clouds forth, I figure I better vacuum after all. Because Greta will stay in the big house for the next few nights, Uncle Jim has gone home for a few days.

The phone rings when I'm on my way to get Garbo. She's at baggage claim; where the hell am I?

"You're supposed to be a half-hour late," I say.

"They made up the time in the air," she says. "Speed demons, these pilots."

"I'm five minutes away. Just wait where you are."

"Not like I can go anywhere," she says, and I swear it is Kale's laugh I hear, loud, right before Garbo hangs up.

I park in the short-term lot. When I walk into the doors by baggage claim, there they are, my favorite people in the world—Greta, Kale, and Sawyer. They each hold up a hand-made posterboard sign. Kale's says "Happy Golden Birthday, Tater Tot!" and Greta's says, "WE LOVE YOU, TATE!" and Sawyer's says, "SEVENTEEN, MY BEAUTY QUEEN." They wave their signs back and forth, the way those guys do when they are hired to lure passersby into a business. *Going out of business sale. Everything must go! Today only, buy one foot-long sub, get the second one FREE!*

It's a spectacle of sincerity, the kind of display you see at airports when a soldier is coming back from Iraq or Afghanistan and the whole family waits with signs, with streamers, with hugs. *Welcome home Johnny!*

"You guys..." They put down their signs and mob me, hug after hug. "You can't have a surprise party at the airport," I say.

"Who says we can't?" says Kale. "We're all here to pick up Garbo, and we just happen to have a cake!"

"And signs," Sawyer says. "No law against carrying posters." Sawyer is distracted. Keeps looking over by the alcove where the bathrooms and water fountain are.

"Beauty queen?" I say.

"Kale came up with that. I was looking for something that rhymed," he says. "But it's true. And it's a line from some song."

"So I guess you don't have to help your dad today."

"Umm, no, that was a white lie," he says. He might as well have a nervous tic, the way he keeps looking over toward the bathrooms.

Kale gives me a big kiss on the cheek, exaggerating the smoochy sound. She shows me a big round Tupperware container with a cake inside.

"Priscilla made it," she says. "Vegan, of course. And chocolate."

"Yum," I say. "Garbo, was this your idea?"

"Kale's, but I was a whole-hog supporter."

Sawyer is now staring at the bathrooms.

"Swimmer Boy!" I say. "You need to go potty?"

Kale snorts.

"Wait one sec," he says, and disappears near potty-land, quickly reappearing with Maddie! She's wearing a sandwich sign. The front says, "Happy Birthday," and Sawyer turns her around in a little dance move, so I can see the back: "to my Big Sister." I can't hold back from tearing up. She is dressed for a party—white ankle socks and black patent leather shoes, a plaid sundress. Her hair is up in a bun. Sawyer lets her go and she runs to me, as fast as she can with the poster board hitting her in the shins.

She's wearing little pearl earrings, and the flower stuck in her bun is a sprig of geranium. "You are so great!" I say. I hug just her neck, the only part of her that's not clad in cardboard. Maddie is all smiles and very few words. I want to protect this girl against all evil for all time.

"How'd you manage this?" I ask Sawyer. I wipe my eyes.

"Mags, from the training? She helped arrange it. We need to have her back to her grandmother by three. I didn't have to *pee*," he says, "I was keeping an eye on your present."

I smile and shake my head, taking it all in. Kale lights candles on the vegan cake, displayed now on a chair in the waiting area.

"Now that may be something we could get in trouble for," says Garbo. "Matches?"

She's right. The nearest security guard is fast on his way over to us.

"Hurry!" Kale says. "Make a wish!" Since the murder, my wish always stays the same. So I wish it and then I blow and just as the guard arrives at our fanfare, the candles are nothing more than some rising smoke and the smell of birthday wax.

He takes the opportunity to scold us anyway. "TSA regulations prohibit fires of any kind on the grounds of the airport."

"It's her birthday," Kale says, pointing at me, and she cuts him a piece of cake, puts it on a paper plate, and hands it to Maddie. "See if the nice policeman wants this."

"No thank you," he says. "Seriously, you kids need to wrap this up and clear out. Is anyone here flying today?"

"Me," Greta says. She raises her hand like she's in class. "I just flew in for my niece's birthday. We're going just as soon as we eat this cake. You sure you don't want a piece?"

He holds his ground, politely. Maddie looks scared, like now we've all gotten ourselves into trouble. What will happen to us now?

"Madoline?" the man says.

Instinctively, I place my arm around her.

"How do you know Maddie?"

"I thought that was you," he says. "I used to be friends with her father...before, you know."

Before *prison*. In my head I fill in the blank.

"Her dad and I worked security together at the university." "You got big," he says to Maddie. She doesn't smile, doesn't recognize him, has no reason to trust him, which I figure is a good thing.

"Go ahead and take your time with the birthday party," he says. "All those years I worked with him, I never knew he had an older kid."

"Oh, Big Brothers Big Sisters," I tell him. "We're not actually related."

"I was about to say...you're the McCoy girl, right?" It's this guy's lucky day for identifying the offspring of felons.

"Yes." I hold out my hand. "Tate—nice to meet you."

"You kids go ahead and enjoy yourselves," he says, all smiley now. "Just don't light any more matches, okay?"

"Roger that," says Kale.

He gives her a look, briefly, like *are you being smart with me? Because if you're being a smartass I can end this shindig now.* But he walks away. Finally, I get to take a bite of the cake Kale's mom made, and it is divine.

Another few flights must've landed because suddenly the baggage claim area is flooded with people, and the carousels start moving. Here come the bags, one by one, through the rubber flap, and Maddie is fascinated. She is more fascinated by the sight of luggage on a conveyor belt than she is by chocolate cake.

"Cool, huh?" I say.

She nods.

"Is this your first time at the airport?"

She nods again.

"Someday maybe you and I will get to go on a trip together," I say, knowing I shouldn't make such promises— but I really do wish it.

I'm busy pressing all the crumbs into the back of my plastic fork, then smearing them into my mouth. I pass the empty paper plate to Kale.

"Another," I say.

"Roger that, birthday girl."

CHAPTER SEVENTEEN:

A Girl Like Her, A Girl Like Me

Being seventeen doesn't change much. Life goes on. School is just a thing to be endured. Weekends fill up with Kale and Sawyer and outings with Maddie. I'm reading a book Greta gave me for my birthday. A collection of essays called *Motherless Daughters* by Hope Edelman. Hope lost her mom when she was a teenager. Cancer. The book is better than therapy, better than making my list of goals and policing myself to achieve them, better than running the whole scenario through my head in an attempt to see in it something I've not seen before. Reading about the experiences of other girls like me who just don't have moms anymore, for all kinds of reasons, turns out to be the bomb. When I finish, I tell my dad about it and he says yes, he knows of Hope Edelman. He says she put together another book after that one—*Letters from Motherless Daughters*. So I go to the big bookstore at the university, and buy that one. For a couple of weeks, I don't watch a single episode of *Dateline* or *48 Hours* or *20/20*. Every night after homework, I am buried in her book. I start composing in my head the letter I could write to Hope Edelman, to her readers, to others like me.

The weather starts to get crappy and Thanksgiving leers at me. Thanksgiving and I don't have a good history.

There was the time my mom got mad at my dad for being critical of how she was doing the turkey. Usually he did it, but she had read something in a magazine and she wanted to try it. It involved putting the bird in a paper bag. My dad was skeptical, since Carla rarely cooked. Why take on an important meal like Thanksgiving? But he took it one step too far—the questioning, the offers to help, the condescension, and Carla, who had already finished most of the Thanksgiving bottle of wine, lost it.

"You want to do it?" she said. "Here." And she took the raw, buttered and salted bird, sage leaves under its skin, and heaved it toward him. Dead poultry doesn't fly well. All fleshy and buttery and slippery. It wasn't a good pass, and it made a human-like thud when it hit the floor.

"Satisfied?" she said.

"Carla," was all he said. She was always disappointing him. I had wanted to see how the bird would come out—to see it through. I wanted her to have the chance to do something right for a change.

That year Mom opted out of Thanksgiving. Dad and I went out to a buffet that had all the traditional foods, but everyone there looked lost or lonely to me. It's a holiday you're supposed to have at home.

After they split up, I alternated who I'd have Thanksgiving with. On my turns with Dad, he experimented with whatever the latest trends were for doing your turkey. Over the years, he tried the brining thing (soaking the bird in salt water in the sink), and the smoking thing (this requires a purchase of a big-ass smoker contraption, and the bird comes out a dark, dusty pink), and even the paper bag thing (the method he'd been so critical of). The turkey was always an experiment—we never established a real tradition. We never said *this is how we do Thanksgiving at our house. This is a McCoy Thanksgiving.* It was always a crap shoot how it would turn out. And we never once focused on what we were thankful for. At the Waggener's, they go around the table three times, each person saying what they are most thankful for.

On the years it was Mom's turn to have me for turkey day, it was worse than a crap shoot. It was guaranteed crap. Ca-ca, you might say, or Boom-boom.

One year, she *forgot* Thanksgiving. She'd been drinking the night before, and out with the guy she was seeing back then. It was noon when I finally woke her up and asked her about the turkey and mashed potatoes and all that. Didn't we need to at least go to the store for some things? I knew turkeys, the big ones, took half the day to cook. Carla looked truly surprised, caught off guard.

"I'm just so tired," she said. "And I have a headache. And it's so late already."

"I have an idea." I dashed to the kitchen.

I ran back to her room, armed with two frozen Swanson's pot pies—one turkey and one beef. "Look what we can have!" I said.

She looked relieved. "That's a good idea, honey. Preheat the oven."

"You can have the turkey one," I said.

"Oh, there aren't two turkeys?"

"No, one is beef."

"Then you'll have the turkey. It's Thanksgiving."

"But Mom," I said, and I was telling the truth, "I actually like beef pot pies way better."

"TATE," she said. "CAN YOU JUST DO ME A FAVOR AND EAT THE TURKEY ONE? SO I WON'T FEEL LIKE A TOTAL FAILURE? PLEASE!"

She said it in that all caps way. I did her that favor. That was Thanksgiving that year.

This year, I can eat a vegan Thanksgiving at Kale's—something called tofurkey, and I am not lying—or I can get a traditional meal at Maddie's grandma's house. Truthfully, what I most want to do is *just skip it*. The vegan thing makes eating anywhere but Kale's awkward. Finally I decide to eat with Maddie because she is, right now anyway, a motherless daughter like me. If I can help her have a better Thanksgiving in her memory bank than I have in mine, well amen to that. I clear it with Kale: I'm going to have to eat some things that I shouldn't because it would be impolite to go and turn everything down. Kale says *go in peace*. She says *let them eat bird*. She says *Godspeed*.

When you're invited to someone's house for dinner, you should bring something to add to the meal. I think of all the usual things—pumpkin pie, green bean casserole, sweet potatoes with melted marshmallows on top. But then I get this other, more original, idea: bring them what they will need for tomorrow's turkey sandwiches. A loaf of sourdough bread from the bakery, a jar of mayonnaise, one of dill pickles, a few tomatoes, and a head of red leaf lettuce.

Maddie's grandma opens the door and the smell of cooking engulfs me. Yum. She takes what I've brought, looks into the bag, and immediately gets it—"For leftovers! Thank you, hon. Call me Gladys." I've seen her before, but just to pick up or drop off Maddie. The house is tiny, only slightly bigger than my guest house, but it's immaculate. Even the kitchen, which is really part of the living room, which appears to also be her bedroom, is tidy even in the midst of Thanksgiving dinner preparations. Nothing spilled on counters. Dishrag hanging from the stove. It's a dishtowel I've seen at my own grandmother's house, and it matches the curtain on the window above the sink. The place is so small that the oven going on all day serves as a furnace. I take it all in. This woman doesn't have much money, but she sure does love this place. It shows. She's a short, solid woman, wearing an apron that has seen a lot of turkey dinners. There's no way she's the one who put the fear of God in Maddie.

Maddie runs up and clamps me around the hips.

"Hey you," I say. She doesn't say anything. Not a word girl, this one.

Gladys says, "Show Miss Tate your room." To me, she says, "She cleaned it!"

Maddie pulls me like my arm is the handle of some red wagon down a short hall and into a room that could be a walk-in closet. No windows and no furniture. She has what looks like a crib mattress taking up most of the floor space. It's been made up fancy into a girly bed—a purple comforter, folded in half, with yellow and white daisies, and ruffles on the edges. "I love the daisies!" I say. "Are these your stuffed animals?"

Maddie nods. "You want to play that game?" she says.

"What game is that?"

"The magic carpet and the animals."

I remember now. "Sure! Which ones are mine?"

She gives me a unicorn, a long, lime green snake, and a teddy bear. She takes the tiger and the lamb. "You take three," I say, "and I'll just have two." She shakes her head.

"You're company," she says.

"Well, okay. Where should we be traveling?"

"We are running away," she says.

"Sounds good."

We give our animals names, and get onto the magic carpet bed.

"I think it's winter," I suggest.

"*Snowy*," she says, smiling.

"*Deep* snow," I add.

"And our babies don't have coats," she says.

"Well, the snake might be cold, but the others have fur, right?"

She considers this, nods.

"Wait," she says, and jumps up and goes to three stacked milk crates in the corner, which hold her clothes. She pulls out a long sock. "For your snake!"

"Excellent," I say. And as I put it over the wiggly green snake, sliding it down his length, I can't help remembering a lesson we had in Health class—the correct application of a condom. If Kale were here right now, we would burst out laughing as I slide this sheath down this um...pet serpent.

"There," I say. I'm smiling.

"Is he warm?"

"He's toasty! Thanks, Maddie."

"What's leafy green?" she says out of the blue, and it's like she knew I was just thinking of Kale.

"You're talking about my friend from the birthday party?"

"You said leafy green."

"That's a nickname I have for her. Kale is a name she gave herself. Her name used to be Karen, but she didn't like it. And she picked Kale because she eats a lot of vegetables and kale is a vegetable she likes, and they call it a leafy green vegetable. So I call her Leafy Green sometimes, just for fun. She calls me things like Tater Tot and Tater Chip."

Maddie doesn't say anything, but I think she understands.

"Did you see the groceries I brought for your grandma?"

She nods.

"Well, that lettuce is also a leafy green. Any vegetable that looks like leaves."

"Like spinach," she says.

"Exactly. Spinach is a well-known leafy green. And kale is an especially tasty leafy green, and it's pretty. Very curly, like Kale's hair, too." Maddie takes everything in. She may not say much, but she's not missing one word of what I tell her.

"Sometimes grown-ups might say to kids, 'Eat your leafy greens!' because they are full of nutrition and good for you."

"And spinach makes you strong," she says. "Like Popeye."

"Exactly. You are very smart."

When our game of magic carpet in the deep snow is just about to get going, we hear the doorbell ring. Maddie gets the same look of fright she had at our picnic. She runs out to the hallway where she can see her grandma open the door to her mom. Uninvited guest.

She looks at me, gives her tiger's tail a twist, and dutifully goes to hug her mother.

Well, this is when it gets interesting, because Gladys has only set three places at the little kitchen table. Maddie's two siblings have recently been farmed out to other relatives, so it's just her and her dad's mother living in this tiny duplex. When Angela, Maddie's mom, sees me and does the math, she says, "Well, I guess there's no room for me."

"I didn't know you were coming," says Gladys. "I can't read minds."

"You know I want to see my kids on the holidays."

"Maddie, add another place setting to the table," Gladys says. She gets a chair from a desk in the main room and puts it at the table. "Well," she says to Angela, "you're just in time. Everything's ready!"

You can tell Grandma Gladys would like to keep things

kind and cordial, and you can tell just as much that Angela would like to have a good turkey day fight. (She would've enjoyed holidays at our house.) She lights up a cigarette and Gladys waves her hand at her. "Not in the house! Please, it'll ruin the taste of the food. Take that outside."

Maddie is quiet, on the watch. She seems to know what to expect from this mom of hers. Angela stubs her cigarette out in the sink, runs water on the nub, and puts it in the trash.

"Well, excuse me for living," she says.

Gladys ignores this and says, "Let's eat!"

"I'm Tate," I say. I hold out my hand but she doesn't shake it. "I'm a volunteer through Big Brothers Big Sisters and I've been taking Maddie out a few times."

"I know who you are," she says. "The McCoy girl from that murder."

I sort of raise my eyebrows, and put my finger to my lips. Surely we don't need to talk to Maddie about murder.

She says, "Oh, now you're going to tell me what I can and can't say around my own daughter?"

"Please," says Gladys, "everyone sit." And we do.

"You wonder why I don't come around; well this is why. All I get are judgments on me." A piece of sweet potato from the serving spoon she's holding splats to the table cloth. "*Shit*," she says. "Maddie, get the sponge!" Maddie jumps from her chair and returns with the sponge. She tries to wipe the clump of potato off the table and into her cupped hand.

"Not like that, stupid! You're just spreading it!" Maddie freezes. I assist. The stain—if it were a paint color at Home Depot—might be called Greasy Squash. I press the wet sponge into it, trying to extract some of the orange.

"Maddie's not stupid," I say. I know I'm putting myself in

the line of fire, but I have to defend Maddie. What kind of a Big would I be if I didn't?

"What are you? Her substitute mother? Is that it?"

"Not at all. I'm just supposed to be a big sister, a friend. I take Maddie out to do fun things," I say. "It's good for both of us because I always wanted a sister and now I have one."

"She *has* a sister and a brother," Angela says. "And maybe I should just go eat at their house, with Uncle Al. They always have enough food."

"We have plenty!" says Gladys. "Please, let's just say grace and eat before it gets cold."

She bows her head. "Heavenly Father above, bless this food to our bodies and our hearts to Christ Jesus. Amen."

Maddie's eyes are shut so tight, they're all wrinkles. I'm not used to saying prayers before meals. Maybe Angela isn't used to this either, as she and I are the only ones who haven't closed our eyes. We glance at each other. She wants a stare-down, but instead I smile. This woman has serious problems. I thought I had problems.

Gladys cuts the turkey and asks me if I like white meat or dark meat. I say I like it all. Maddie passes me the mashed potatoes and gravy and I send the green beans around toward Angela. She takes them, passes, takes the next dish from me, passes, and it seems for a minute maybe we're over the worst of it and we're just going to have us a Thanksgiving meal. I'm secretly thrilled to have a day off from vegan restrictions. I'm eyeing the soft stick of butter on a saucer, thinking how I will push a fat slice into my potatoes.

Angela says, "If Earl was here, he'd certainly get better treatment than this." Earl must be Maddie's dad, Gladys' son.

"Please," says Gladys. "Have you heard from him?"

"He called me last week. He's clean four months now."

"One good thing about jail," Gladys says.

Maddie looks back and forth between them.

"This turkey is delicious," I say.

There is a melted yellow lake in the center of my mashed spuds. I am in butter heaven.

Maddie blurts out, "I want to keep living with Grandma." She must think the arrival of her mother means she'll have to go away with her, this woman who has taken up residence in some nearby town, but hasn't kept in touch. Gladys is preferable, anyone can see that.

"Well that's nice, isn't it?" Angela says. "Did I say anything about taking you with me? No."

She takes her plateful of food to the counter and sticks it in the microwave. "I can take a hint," she says. "I'll take my meal and go." The microwave dings and she gets foil out of a drawer. She makes fanfare, tearing off a piece and covering her dish. Next, she cuts right into the pumpkin pie, without asking. Takes half, drops it in a Tupperware container, and forces the lid on. Pumpkin oozes out of one corner. She wipes at it with her finger, licks it off. She pulls two Diet Pepsis from the fridge, and puts one in each jacket pocket.

"See if I come back here again to be treated like dirt."

She turns to Maddie. "And as for you, I don't even want you with me. I wouldn't take you back if you begged me."

Oh boy. I look down at my plate.

Gladys seems unruffled—maybe she's accustomed to these displays. She chews on a mouthful of green beans and mashed potatoes, but she doesn't stop looking at Angela. She's practiced.

"Suit yourself," she says after swallowing. "Enjoy the pie."

I get up to open the door for Angela—her hands are all tied up.

"And you," she says to me. "I don't want my girl with the child of a murderer."

"My father's innocent," I say, but she is already halfway

out the door and doesn't turn back.

Maddie says a timid "Bye." I close the door, and Maddie starts to cry.

Gladys pats Maddie on the knee. "You don't worry about her. You just enjoy your supper."

I give Maddie a long, sideways hug. Wiping at her eyes, she says, "Who's a murderer?"

Gladys says, "Nobody. And you don't need to worry about that." To me, Gladys says, "It's the drugs that make her that way." She shakes her head.

"Who wants to put their plate in the microwave for a stretch?" she says.

We all do. Maddie helps me do them in turn.

"Well," I say. "Angela seems very tense."

"Oh, that was nothing. She was on her best behavior because we have company." Gladys turns to me and mouths the word "abusive." The thought of it makes me feel sick.

Maddie smiles now, happy the mean mother is gone, the food is newly warm, and there's still half a pie to look forward to.

I like Gladys. She puts up with a lot of nonsense in order to be a good grandma to Maddie. And even with the surprise visit, this was a pretty good Thanksgiving overall. Without a doubt, the best bird I ever ate.

Maddie leans over her plate, trying to get a bite of sweet potato in her mouth without losing any of it. A lock of hair falls forward and mixes in with the forkful of sticky, marshmallowy mush. "Here," I say, and push the hair back behind her ear. "Now go for it." And she does.

"I'm saving one green bean for my snake," I say to her.

She lights up, remembering. "I'm saving turkey for my tiger!"

"They have a long magic carpet ride ahead of them!" I say.

Maddie nods, her signature move, a girl who's learned to

go along with things, to not spill, to say yes, to be invisible. In the history of bad family holidays, there is bad and there is worse, and I have never had it as bad as Maddie does. I want to be the best Big I can possibly be. I make a mental note to be sure that, after dessert and dishes, we finish our game of magic carpet. A game like that can save a girl like her, a girl like me.

CHAPTER EIGHTEEN

WHEN THE WEATHER IS COLD

Kale and Sawyer and I swim at the heated indoor pool when the weather is cold. Barton Springs is open year-round and there are hard-core swimmers who do laps there in winter, but we think that's nuts. At the indoor pool, everyone has their own roped off lane, so you don't bump into anyone, but we all prefer Barton Springs. This will keep us in shape till we're ready to brave it again in the spring.

This week we schedule swimming for after the court stuff—the informant guy has been called to testify and Sawyer needs to be there. Kale and I ride our bikes in an effort to beat the winter blues. Just because we *can* drive doesn't mean we have to; people get lazy and too comfortable. Kale's talking about this again as we pedal. Just as she's making her point—*cars insulate you from the world you're traveling through. You don't feel the environment*—a truck rattles by through a large puddle. Brown water drenches us and we scream, first from the shock of the wet and the cold, but then in anger. Kale gives the guy the finger as I call out, "Thanks, asshole!"

"Shit," I say.

"Damn," she says. We are soaked from the hips down. Kale says, "I was planning on swimming *later*, at the pool."

"What was that you were saying again? About how the evil automobile insulates its passenger?"

She laughs, then says, "Shut up."

As we're getting back on our bikes, Sawyer pulls over and rolls down his window.

"Want a ride?"

We're only a couple blocks away—not worth the time it would take to remove the front wheels and cram both bikes into the back of his mom's Honda CRV.

"You okay?" I say to Sawyer. He looks worried.

"Fine," he says, too fast. "See you there in a sec, then." And he's off, slowly, careful not to spray us with even a drop of street suds.

"That was weird," Kale says. "Very business-like for Swimmer Boy."

"I think he's Reporter Boy right now, that's what I think."

At the pool, there's a wait for getting a lane. This town has a lot of swimmers in it, and they're all here today. Right away, one guy finishes and Kale takes the lane. This leaves me and Sawyer sitting alone by the pool.

"What happened at the trial? Spit it out."

"It's nothing that happened," he says. "It's just a feeling I have, a hunch, and it's not good."

"You can tell me. You *have* to tell me. I rely on you for my information."

"But it's not something that's come out. Yet. I don't know. It's just a sense I have." He rolls his towel into a tight torpedo, tucking in the ends.

I don't say anything. He'll talk, he just has to do it in his own time. He whips the towel out in front of him again, folds it, and rolls it up again.

"Please stop punishing the towel."

Reporter Boy is more serious than Swimmer Boy, but I get a chuckle. And he lets go of the towel.

"It's not good," he says. "And I'm not sure you'd want to know."

"None of this is something anyone would *want*, Sawyer. But I've been managing the facts, so just tell me."

"It's not fact, that's what I'm saying. It's a feeling."

A lane opens up and Sawyer looks like he's been saved. "Wait," I say. I tell the woman behind us she can go ahead. "I'm not going to swim a mile wondering what you're not telling me."

He spits it out. Based on what was revealed today, he is starting to doubt the validity of the tip. Based on what he heard today, it is starting to feel like someone made that whole thing up.

"Why? What'd they say?"

"Well, for one, that guy who is the supposed real killer? He's dead. Suicide."

"He killed himself when he thought he'd been found out?"

"No. He killed himself over a year ago. This is what I'm saying. I think the guy who made the call was put up to it, and I think they purposely accused someone who couldn't go to prison for the crime, because he was dead. It's like whoever planned this whole tip thing had *some* scruples. *Some* inability to put another man in prison for life. So this guy was convenient, because he's gone. But he did date your mom, really briefly, a year or so before her murder."

"But he killed himself not long after her murder. Maybe

he did do it, and committed suicide out of guilt."

"There are lots of theories going around. He killed himself because he couldn't live with what he'd done; he killed himself out of heartbreak."

"Over Carla?"

"Some people are thinking that. Like maybe she didn't want to keep dating him and maybe he was really in love with her or something. Things like that happen."

"So what's your hunch?"

"They had the guy's psychiatrist testify today. The man had a history of suicide attempts, and the shrink feels he was finally determined enough to be successful. He'd dealt with clinical depression his whole adult life, but he wasn't capable of a crime like this. Tortured by his disease, but not a threat to others, basically."

Another lane opens and we wave people from the line behind us on.

"My dad is also not capable of a crime like this." I'm suddenly really hot, then really cold, like when you have the flu.

"I know," Sawyer says. "That's why I'm confused. At the risk of you hating me for saying this...I have a feeling it's going to come out that your dad had someone make that call, that it was all fabricated. That he paid someone off to do it. And he knew somehow that this guy had killed himself, so he was thinking he could divert the attention away from himself as prime suspect, but wouldn't have to live with the guilt of sending some innocent man to prison for life. The guy who killed himself—the fact that he dated your mom—he was convenient."

The tile walls look wavy, the same as the surface of the water. I feel like I could fall down from dizziness, everything turning to liquid. It's the opposite of buoyancy.

"I have to swim," Sawyer says. "I need to swim really bad.

I'm going to take the next lane." His arms are folded across his bare chest. "Kale's going to finish before we even get started." He shifts from foot to foot. What he's said, makes me feel sick, like I have a plague, and he doesn't seem like a friend to trust right now.

I say, "Please just tell me what you're thinking."

"I'm thinking if your dad made that whole thing up...I hate to think what that might mean."

I hate to think that too, but I refuse to think any such thing. "You know what?" I say. "I'm going home."

"Tate, you know I'm on your side. You know I've believed from the beginning he was innocent."

"I have to go. I feel sick."

"You're not there in the courtroom all those hours; stuff transpires and things change and I can't help what I feel. I didn't want to tell you, but you asked. You pressed. And now you're mad."

"You can't be on my side and also think this way, Sawyer. The two things are contradictory."

The walls keep swimming and buckling and my stomach would like to hurl. When another lane opens up, Sawyer says, "I'm going to swim." He hugs me, but I don't hug back. He might as well be hugging a tightly rolled up towel. He fixes his goggles and dives in, leaving me. *Mom, Dad, Jasper, now Sawyer?* As I watch him slice through the blue water, his body buoyant there, just beneath the surface, I feel myself sinking. I feel myself drown.

Kale stands dripping beside me, goose-bumped.

"How is it you're not even wet?" she says.

"We're leaving."

"Why? What about Sawyer?"

"Come on." I give her a look: we'll discuss this later.

To keep up with me on the way home, Kale has to be in race mode.

She catches up only once. "Tate, what happened? Why are we in such a hurry?" Beside me, she sees the tears streaming backwards in the wind. We ride the rest of the way in silence.

CHAPTER NINETEEN:

MERRY CHRISTMAS

It's only two days before Sawyer's suspicions are confirmed. It's all over the news; it's a game-changer. The anonymous phone tip was orchestrated by Arthur McCoy himself. The caller? *A guy who was never even in jail!* A former member of the janitorial crew at The Center for the Family, a former employee of the defendant.

I knew this man, and recognize his picture in the paper: Ed Halloway. He used to let me steer the big push broom down the main hallway at The Center. I'd go there after school on nights I stayed with my dad, do my homework till Dad was finished seeing clients. Ed's family had been some of the first clients of The Center, while his wife went through chemo. The goal of The Center was to identify needs in families, especially low income ones, and provide whatever services were needed to help keep those families together. The Center was founded on the idea that family is sacred. Ed's family got free child-care, transportation to and from chemo, emergency loans. His janitor job helped him pay the medical bills. Ed Halloway and his family were the first big case The Center took on, and got a lot of publicity. He loved my dad, was indebted to him.

He caved on the witness stand. What nice guy wouldn't? I hate what my father put him through. It's like the priests who molest the little altar boys and then tell them it's God's will—and if they tell anyone, God will punish them. Do you follow your own conscience, or do you follow the lead of your former boss, your friend, your idol, the man who helped you through trying times? My dad could've talked Ed into anything.

Sawyer leaves me a string of voicemails. He's sorry. He wants to see me. He wants to be there for me. He knows how hard this must be. He wishes none of it were true. He misses me. Can we talk?

I can't hold the facts against him. Just because he figured it out before everyone else did—he's not responsible for it. The part I can't get past is what he alluded to: *if this is true, I hate to think what it might mean.* Everyone's thinking it. Artie McCoy isn't who we thought he was. He set up the tip that would lead to his own release and another man's conviction. He's dishonest, and if he's that, no telling what else he might be. A murderer? Sure. You'd be surprised at the conclusions people jump to. The same people who posted letters to the editor in the paper, praising my father and his work and expressing shock at the insinuation that this man might've done this heinous thing to the mother of his own child. Now they'll write to the paper expressing more shock: *who among us would ever have thought Arthur McCoy capable of this unspeakable act?* Comments will pour in over the e-waves—everyone *knew* there was something shady about that guy all along!

I think it's safe to say that people in this town are now as sure of his guilt as they once were of his innocence. And the court's about to take a long recess for Christmas. If my dad is going to pull out of this hole he's dug, it's not going to happen till after the new year.

What's really hard is going through this worst case of sce-narios without Swimmer Boy. I don't think I'd realized until now how inseparable we've become, how much I use him as a sounding board, how I talk to him as openly as I talk to Kale or Greta. Forget about finding him adorable—he was becom-ing my best friend. But there's a war going on, and he's just joined forces with the enemy.

I need to go talk to my father.

I'm numb as I go through the usual frisk routine, like I'm seeing everything through a dirty window. I'm on auto-pilot, talking to the guards like nothing's new, but we all know that's not the case. As I wait for them to bring Dad in, I try for a second to tap into our old telepathy. *What is he thinking right now? What in God's name was he thinking when he hatched this horrible plan?*

He walks in, saying, "How's my favorite daughter?" I don't say anything. "What is it, honey?"

"Dad, do you really have to ask?" I'm caught off guard by how I feel, looking at him in his jail uniform. I've spent so much time building up an immunity to all this, but in this moment, everything floods down at once and I'm crying.

"Sweetheart." He tries to hug me but I pull away.

"Tate. This doesn't change anything."

I dredge a wadded-up tissue out of my jacket pocket, and wipe my nose.

"How can you say that? Now, even when you're acquitted of the murder charge, they'll get you for perjury and obstruc-tion of justice. I heard them say that, Dad, on the news."

Dad says, "Sit down, honey. You're distraught."

I sit, then quickly stand up. "I don't wanna sit! Why have I always been so damn obedient?" I don't like anything about me or him in this moment. He looks at me from a professional distance, the way he used to look at Mom.

"Stop observing me!" I stand behind the chair, leaning on its back. My insides tell me I have to be in motion. I turn the chair around and lean my butt on the back, but the chair squeaks away from me. I turn around, pick the chair up, and bang it back down on the floor, like I'm showing it who's boss. An image of a lion tamer comes to my mind. They use chairs to protect themselves, too. But my dad's no lion. He just sits there in his chair, identical to the one I'm alternately promenading around and abusing. He looks like a normal dad; I look like the lion in need of taming. Finally, I swing the chair around and straddle it backwards. I take a breath.

"There," Dad says. "Comfy?"

"Dad! Stop avoiding the subject! You know what everyone out there is thinking right now? They think if you did that—that lie—then you're not who they thought you were. People who were so sure of your innocence don't know anymore. Even my friends, Dad!" And that starts me off crying again.

Dad tries to take my hand but I won't have it.

"I'm sorry you're upset, Tate, and I'm sorry if I've disappointed you, but you can't know what this is like unless you've stood in my shoes for the past eighteen months." He looks down at his own feet when he says "shoes." What they wear in jail is more like slippers. "I want out of here, and I want to resume my life. Our life."

My dad has this way of coming across like he's without flaws or faults, like some perfect egg built out of Play-Doh. He sits across from me with that expression on his face, the same one I know was hard for my mom. He always got to play the part of the kind, patient, reasonable one.

"You're the one who should be crying, Dad. You messed up. Would you just admit for once that you made a really huge mistake?"

Dad says, "The execution was sloppy, I'll give you that. Ed couldn't handle the pressure."

"He couldn't lie under oath, you know that. I'm asking you to admit *you* were wrong."

My father thinks for a few moments. "I exhibited poor judgment, imagining this could be pulled off. But the fact remains, I need to get out of here any way I can."

"So you can't say you made a mistake?"

He does this thing where he puts his head down and rubs both eyebrows simultaneously, with thumb and middle finger. Kale and I joke about this—we imitate the move when we want to surreptitiously give someone the finger.

"I tried something, Tate, with good intentions, and it didn't work. But I don't see it as a *mistake*. It was a means to an end."

"Okay," I say. "I'm gonna go."

I walk toward the door where I see, through the Plexiglas, red and green tinsel garlands up and down the hallway, the decorated tree at the end of the hall.

I turn back. "Merry Christmas," I manage, before a flash flood of emotion clogs my throat again.

CHAPTER TWENTY:

To Be Jolly

Uncle Jim tells me, three days before Christmas, that we are selling the house—studio and all. The house my mom lived in will also go on the market, once it's emptied, but Jim tells me it will be hard to sell. No one wants to buy a house where someone was murdered.

"We've avoided it as long as we can, Tate, and with these recent developments, there's no way around it anymore."

He explains the finances—how all this time we haven't had Dad's income, how Dad was paying two mortgages, this one and the one for Mom's house. *And* he'd given up the rental income on my studio.

"I don't have to tell you he did that for you, Tate."

This is Jim's forte—making people feel guilty.

He says I have no idea how much the legal fees are adding up to—he's taken a second mortgage on his own home and on Grampa's condo, and all that money is already gone.

"It's astronomical," he says, "what this is costing. The only sane thing to do is put both houses on the market. We simply need to turn these assets into cash." Uncle Jim enjoys using words like "asset."

I nod. I get it. I'm not stupid.

"And you're probably wondering about now," he says, "what this will mean for you." *Wow, Jimbo, you read my mind. Gee, you must be psychic.* He pauses for dramatic effect.

"Well," he says. "We've given that a bit of thought. It's not our intention to uproot you or put you through any more than you've already been through. You only have one year of high school left after this one." *Somebody's done his homework!* "Once you go to college, wherever you end up going, that's where you'll live." *Firm grasp of the obvious, Jimbo.* "You'll be eighteen, you'll be independent. But if the house sells quickly, well, we'll just have to cross that bridge when we get to it. I mean, you'd go to family...you could live with me and Aunt Lucy in Detroit."

As if.

"I'm finishing high school in Austin." I say this calmly, as though it's just a fun fact I'm sharing.

He puts his hand up in a stop sign gesture. "Hear me out."

"I'm not moving," I say. "If you sell the studio out from under me, I'll move in with Kale's family."

"The girl with the vegetable name? What kind of parents let their kid do that? It's embarrassing."

"Kale has terrific parents, FYI. I'd have been lucky to get parents like John and Priscilla."

"Fair enough. I shouldn't judge."

"You shouldn't. Because the Waggeners are great."

"But Tate, we can't ask them to take you in for that long. They have their own kids to feed and bills to pay and we don't know what their financial picture looks like. It's a lot to ask of someone who isn't family."

"If it has to be family, I'd go live with Greta."

Jimbo says, "Wrong family."

"What are you talking about?"

"You know all this, Tate. Your mother has been nothing but trouble for your father, from the moment they met. But what it's come to now—all this—this trial—things your father should never be dealing with. I know you like Greta, but she *is* Carla's sister and at this point, we don't want to involve *that family* in ensuring your wellbeing."

"She's nothing like Carla—they didn't even get along. It's not her fault. And besides, I'm not moving."

Jim walks out, saying, "We'll talk when you've calmed down."

"I'm CALM!"

I call Kale: voicemail. I call Greta: voicemail.

I would call Sawyer but he's not an option anymore. *Can we all bow our heads and have a moment of sadness about this?*

Will somebody please answer their damn phone? I'm at maximum capacity of what I can take. I've been *cooperating* for so long, trying to prove how *okay* I am, but if they make me move, I will not be okay.

I open the window that faces the big house. "I AM NOT OKAY!" I tell the whole world, and then the tears start. The enormity of all I have to cry about could produce tears enough for a lap pool.

"And I'm not moving!" I shout into the yard. I'm sobbing, pathetic gasps for breath. I shut the window, hard, like that might stop the flood.

And then I see her, the woman from *Dateline*. Pauline something or other. She's getting out of a gold Prius and she has her notebook and her video camera. She's wearing spike heels. As she crosses the yard toward the guest house, a heel sticks in the wet ground and her foot comes out. She balances herself with one nylon-stockinged foot onto the mud.

I open the window again.

"Please go away," I say, not mean, not nice, just a plea. She's made it to the front step and proceeds to knock and knock and knock, and I proceed to not answer.

The case does a nosedive. The lawyers for the defense want out. They feel my father's fabrication of evidence has made mockery of their efforts. People question whether this jury can be objective now. It's the end of the year; people are tired. Everyone wants to go home and forget about Arthur McCoy and his lies. They want to have their Christmas.

There are rumors that it'll be a mistrial, that it will all start over—new judge, new lawyers, fresh jury—in the new year.

And then this: I get a call from Mags at Big Brothers Big Sisters. She says it breaks her heart to tell me this—*then please, don't tell me*—but Maddie's father has made it clear that he doesn't want Maddie seeing me anymore. He doesn't want his kid with the kid of some guy in jail.

"But *he's* in *prison*!" I say.

Mags says, "I know. It sounds hypocritical. But felons can be very judgmental about other felons."

"But my dad's innocent. Not that I can expect you or anyone to believe that at this point."

"I know," she says. "But what your father is accused of … we have to abide by Maddie's family's wishes."

"Gladys likes me. Can we ask her?"

"Unfortunately, she doesn't have legal guardianship. What the dad says, goes."

Mags says we should wait till this whole case is resolved before we try to match me up with another Little. I don't say this to Mags, but even if she assigned me to some other girl, I wouldn't want to do it. Not yet, anyway. It's like if your dog gets lost and you replace him with a new dog right away. You should feel the absence, honor the missing dog. You want to be there and dogless, should the lost pet come back to you. I want to wait for Maddie.

Our cat, Bellboy, hasn't been seen since the night of the murder. We don't know if he ran away out of fear, or if the murderer took him to live somewhere else. We just don't know. Bellboy knows what happened that night. I still think sometimes that he might show up on my mom's property, rubbing himself against the back steps.

For weeks after the murder, Jasper and I checked the animal shelter for Bellboy. We put up Lost Cat flyers on every telephone and street light in that neighborhood. I made it my mission to find my poor cat, who had no doubt been traumatized by what he'd witnessed. I wanted to comfort him. I wanted him to comfort me.

One psychiatrist I was seeing back then, a trauma specialist, said that I was disassociating from my mother's murder through my obsession with finding the cat. Excellent theory, Doctor Dildo, but did it ever occur to you, it's just normal to want my cat back?

When Mom and Dad had split up, Bellboy went with Mom. I was mad at my mom back then, refusing to believe I missed her, but I missed Bellboy madly. On the rare occasions Mom went on trips, Bellboy came to stay with me and Dad. He's a snuggly, long-haired cat, the color of hay. I lost Mom, I lost Bellboy, and now I'm losing Maddie.

Mags offers me a paying job until I can volunteer again. I can help with training, I can help in the thrift store, I can work in the office, answering phones and processing paperwork. It occurs to me that getting a part-time job is the only thing left on my list. She tells me to come around the Monday after New Year's and she'll get me set up.

I don't have illusions about Christmas resembling Christmas. *'Tis the season to be jolly*. Like Thanksgiving, this is something I'd rather just skip. *Fa-la-la-la-la, la-la-la-la*. It's not like I expect to receive anything, but it would be nice if people stopped taking stuff away.

CHAPTER TWENTY-ONE:

EVERY UNSAD THING

Maybe it's me "disassociating" again, but I cannot accept this news about Maddie—that we're not allowed to spend time together anymore. Kale and I put our heads together. We're at the mall where she's buying last minute Christmas stuff for her parents.

"It's not cool," she says. "They should know better than to cut this whole thing off without allowing you to at least say goodbye to her."

"Totally," I say.

"I mean, it goes against everything that Big Brothers Big Sisters stands for! Isn't it like their mission to give kids from troubled backgrounds an adult who will be guaranteed to be a positive, stable influence?"

"Yes," I say. "But that's the whole thing. They're saying I'm a bad influence."

"That is the biggest pile of dog dookie I have ever heard of. Like you could ever be a bad influence! I wish this had happened when Bower was making us write those argumentative essays. I would've totally written about this." Kale wrote an argument in favor of veganism; I wrote mine on how gays should be allowed in Boy Scouts.

Kale is just ranting, but her rants are brilliant. She comes up with the most perfect ideas. "We'll do it!" I say. "We will write an argumentative essay, in the form of a letter, to Big Brothers Big Sisters of Austin, making the case that what they've done to me and Maddie contradicts the very philosophy their organization was founded on!"

"You are so right," says Kale. "We need to go home and fact-check. Do our research."

"As Bower would say, we have to come across as informed and educated and fair in our assessment. And we have to concede something to the opposition."

"Logos and pathos and all that Greek garbage."

"Don't forget ethos," I tell her. Just having a plan makes me feel better. Kale thinks we can't waste any time; it has to hit them during the holidays, so they will feel the ethos of the Christmas season. After making our case, we'll ask for something specific and quantifiable. We'll ask that I get to see Maddie one more time, to give her a Christmas gift. Which sets us off on a new mission: finding the perfect gift for Maddie.

Thinking of Bellboy, I suggest a pet, something small and unobtrusive, something Gladys won't mind. Kale says goldfish—I am thinking turtle. We head to the pet store. We look at those fish you have to be careful of because they will eat the other fish in the tank. We look at the cats, stuck in their one-square-foot cages. We consider parakeets and guinea pigs. Tiny white mice—Gladys might not be a fan.

Undecided, we go to the food court, where a vegan's only choices are French fries or Chinese vegetables. Kale goes for veggies; I stick with good ol'fries. The place is packed—two shopping days till Christmas—and we have to wait for a table.

While squirting ketchup all over my fries, I'm struck with a brilliant idea. The bookstore! We can introduce Maddie to the joys of literature. We can help her, as Bower helped us, to see everything going on beneath the surface of a story.

I share this lightbulb moment of mine with Kale, and she says, appropriately, "Eureka, Tate Worm. Like Book Worm, get it?"

"Good one," I say. "What book though?" And then it hits us. A book we adored when we were her age, one we took turns checking out from the library. *The Secret Language*, by Ursula Nordstrom. It's about this friendship between two girls at boarding school. They develop a secret language, kind of like me and Kale with our salutations. Together, these two girls make boarding school not just bearable, but they actually start having fun. It was my mother who first found the book at the library and thought I would like it.

"God," I say. "I want to reread it now!"

"Let's just hope they have it." Kale empties a soy sauce packet onto her plate and pops a miniature corn cob into her mouth.

The bookstore has one copy, glowing there on the shelf. And the letter we write to Big Brothers Big Sisters (Kale is killer at argumentation) has the desired effect. They not only applaud our effort in pointing out their hypocrisy, they set up an appointment for me on December 30th, to meet Maddie at the office, where Mags will be officiating and Gladys will also be present. The higher-ups at the Bigs office agree that closure is a good idea.

On the 28th, in preparation, I write Maddie a note and stick it inside the book. I use the comics section of the newspaper to wrap it up. My mom used to do that—she cared about recycling and reusing. Plus, those pages are colorful and fun, and while I know this closure of ours will have some sadness in it, I want to make it as fun as possible.

Kale gives me a ride over there and waits in the car. As I walk from the car to the building, I make a wish and send it out into the winter air, that Maddie will one day soon have a best friend the quality of Leafy Green. A friendship as rare as the girls' in *The Secret Language*, to lift her out of her circumstances. As I pull hard on the door, I look back toward Kale and she blows me a kiss.

Maddie runs to me and hugs me around the waist. I do my best not to cry, but partings are not my forte. I haven't known Maddie all that long, and we've only seen each other maybe eight times, but I've needed someone to take care of. I've needed someone to protect. By taking care of Maddie, it's like indirectly, I'm taking care of me.

I find myself wishing I'd brought her more—everything Kale and I had pondered. I'd like to present her with a goldfish and a turtle. A guinea pig and some mice. A cage of colorful, chattering parakeets. A small zoo of animals to love.

"Hey," I say. "Let's sit over here." She lets me lead her by the hand over to some chairs. Mags and Gladys try to stay out of our way. "This is for you," I say, once we're sitting as close as we can scoot the chairs.

"Thank you," she says.

"Go ahead and open it." Maddie looks over to her grandmother, who nods her head. She pulls off the newspaper, crumbles it up, and hands it to me. She examines the picture on the front cover of the two girls. My note to her is in there, on pink lined paper, folded up to the size of a Post-it. She looks at me for permission to unfold it, but I say, "Why don't you read that later, when you get home?" She nods and tucks it inside her knee sock. She's wearing Christmas socks—green with reindeer on them.

"Wow," I say, "I love your socks."

Maddie just smiles.

"You know my friend Leafy Green?"

"Kale," she says.

"Yup. Well, this book was our favorite book when we were your age. We read it over and over. I think you're going to love it, too."

Maddie turns some pages, in search of the illustrations.

"So," I tell her, trying to think of every unsad thing in the world in my attempt not to cry, "put that note in a safe place and I want you to read it every single time you miss me, or you're sad, or someone hurts your feelings, or you're just sad, or your mom does something mean, or kids at school act like creeps, or you're sad..." My repetition of the one phrase makes her laugh. Maddie could turn out to be a word girl, after all, coming up with her own secret language of survival.

CHAPTER TWENTY-TWO:

LIKE A SMALL PREGNANCY

A card from Sawyer comes in the mail—part apology, part Happy New Year. At the end, he puts *All the best* and *Toodles* and then, *Sawyer, AKA Swimmer Boy. P.S. What are your plans for JANUARY????* I want to call him more than anything.

I start a new list of goals—call them New Year's resolutions, but first I rip the old ones off the wall. They reek of Swimmer Boy now, even though, when I wrote them, I didn't even know him. The old goals, all accomplished, don't make me feel one bit happier. It's January and I'm without Sawyer. It's a new year in which my mother is still dead, my father is still the prime suspect, the house is up for sale, and my little sister has been taken away from me.

On January 13th, which would've been my mom's 48th birthday, we're having a big pottery sale, slash memorial, slash benefit. Greta and her sister Meg have been planning this for a while, but now that both houses are about to go on the market, we have no choice but to clean out my mom's pottery studio. Aunt Meg makes sculptures out of found objects and vintage kitchen items and old game pieces and you name it. She's a good resource, since she's been in the art world, knows how things should be priced. There's what the piece is worth and then there's the add-on for the fact of it being a benefit. People come to such a thing knowing that if they make a purchase, they are donating to whatever the benefit is benefitting. (This one is benefitting me—College Fund for the Motherless Daughter.) On top of that, the artist is no longer living, so the work that is for sale takes on a rarity. Greta wants me to go to my mom's studio and choose a few pieces. They don't want to sell something that I might want. Greta's already gone over, the last time she was in town, and taken what she liked. I could've gone with her, but I didn't.

Going to her studio is no small matter. I'd planned to do it that week before she died; *it was on my list*. What, I wonder now, could possibly have been more important? Why didn't I visit her there while she was alive? It could've been a new phase of our relationship. It could've been a place to start. It could've given me something more to remember.

I procrastinated back then and I'm procrastinating now. Greta made me promise to do it before they get here for the benefit. I've left it to the last possible day.

I overthink every aspect. Should I drive, bike or walk? Or take the city bus? Will I need the car to carry back whatever I decide to keep? How big is this stuff? How heavy? Should I bike and bring a backpack? Some bubble wrap?

Finally, I decide to ride my bike, for the meditative aspects of it. Pedaling can be like swimming. You go and go and go and since it's more physical than mental, your mind isn't involved, and it can wander. I've thought through many

things on long bike rides. For instance: I've fantasized ad nau-
seum my first kiss with Swimmer Boy.

I fill my daypack with a few towels for wrapping up the
goods. It's cold out, so I put on a long underwear shirt, a
fleece, and then a bright yellow windbreaker. The windbreaker
ensures drivers can see me—a bicycling bumble bee.

If I had my way I would mosey over there, delaying the
arrival, but it's knife-slicing cold and my fingers are numb
even through the gloves. I have no choice but to ride as fast
as I can.

This is the closest I've been to where it all happened, and it
hits me all at once—my mother was murdered in that house.
If the murder had happened in her pottery studio, I would
not be over here, doing this. The key is where Greta said it
would be, inside a planter by the back door. The plant, whatever it was, is now brown stalks of dry nothing. The edges of
the dead leaves are crisp and sharp. The last person to use the
key pushed it into the hard dirt and I have to dig to free it. I
wipe it on my jeans, blow on it to keep any dirt from messing
up the lock. I look in a window that has messy fingerprints on
it, my mother's, where she must've pushed it open, hands wet
with clay. The room, even unlit, looks like a happy place—fun,
small enough to be a child's playhouse.

It wasn't always an art studio. For the previous owner, it
had been a boathouse. I remember vividly an argument Carla
and Dad had when he was buying her this house. She wanted
the previous owner to pay to run the water line out to the
studio. Back then, I think everyone thought she might have
her own one-chair salon back there. She'd need a bathroom
for clients to use, and a deep sink for washing hair, rinsing
out dye.

As far as I know, no one ever got shampooed back there in
that boat hangar. Or cut or permed or colored or blown dry.

But the sink came in handy for keeping clay wet and washing up. The bathroom allowed her to work in there all day if she wanted, without having to go in the main house. It strikes me that this little studio meant as much to her as mine does to me. A space all her own. A space where she could totally be herself.

But that day of their disagreement, my father wanted to close the deal, not make any demands of the current owner. He had Mom on speaker phone. She argued that now was the only time they'd have negotiating power. Once they owned the house, adding water to the back would be at their expense.

"Your expense," my dad corrected. Once the house was in his name, he'd pay the mortgage, nothing more. That was the agreement. He only had to provide her a house in the same town until I turned eighteen. Joint custody. If she wanted to turn it into a beauty parlor, well that would be at her own expense.

I distinctly remember wanting to take her side. *Just do it, Dad. Just say yes.* They want to sell the house; they'll do this reasonably small adjustment. I remember thinking, *Why's he being so stubborn? She's actually making sense for once.*

I was on the verge of saying, "Geez Dad, just agree for once," when Carla said, "Jesus Artie, why do you have to be such a dick?" Dad looked at me, switched the speaker phone button off, and took the rest of the call in his study. Sometimes I think he liked fighting with her; he usually won.

I wish I'd spoken up before he shut me out of the conversation. I remember thinking, *She's right, he is being a total dick.*

Peering in the windows from all four sides of this shed, all I can think is, *Well, she got her way in the end.* Water to the back house. Some part of Dad still wanted to give her whatever she wanted. I don't think he ever got over how hard he fell in love with her.

Eventually it's too cold to continue this voyeur's approach. I knock on the door. (Weird, I know, but it seems proper.) I pause. I put the key in the lock, turn it, and push the door open.

The stale air in the closed-up room rushes to replace itself. Immediately I smell her, taste her. Feel the dust of airborne clay on my forearms, like pollen. I plug in a space heater and turn it on. It puts out a smell of something burning.

First, I'm drawn to the art—shelves and shelves so full of it that things have to be stacked to fit. Bowls nest inside each other. Dinner plates—there must be four dozen—have been stacked on the floor according to the color of their glaze. There are cups and mugs—some wheel-thrown, others hand-built. Sizes range from teensy to huge. A shallow, quarter-sized bowl—something you'd have by the bed to put your earrings in at night, or by the sink to drop a ring in before doing dishes. Bowls big enough for sauces or salsa. An array of small bowls for salt and pepper, tiny clay spoons inside. I know they're for salt, because Carla set one up as a display, with salt and pepper inside and, resting on the edge, a tiny Alice in Wonderland spoon—the most intricate, delicate, baby spoon you've ever seen, the curve of the spoon's bowl holding a fraction of Carla's fingerprint.

One shelf is filled with pitchers and vases—crude-looking farmhouse pitchers with sturdy, handmade handles— you imagine the pitcher filled with milk just squeezed from a cow. Small pitchers, in sets with sugar bowls. More adorable spoons sitting inside.

And the glazes! The variety! How is it that I've not known how fun this could be? To make things out of clay, to pick color combos like I did for the studio walls, and decide on the finish—something shiny or matte? Smooth surface or grainy like dirt? I test several mugs for how well they fit, my finger looping through the handle, my thumb protectively perched on top. How well would this cup or that cup fit my mouth? My particular sip? I try a few out, bringing them up to my lips, kissing theirs.

In one mug, there's an angel painted on the bottom, inside. When you finish your coffee or tea, there she is—a winged, cherubic thing. She's yellow and white and the cup's glaze is a deep blue and I know this is one thing I want for myself. I turn it over and read *C. Robichaux*. She'd gone back to her maiden name? When did she drop the McCoy? All the news reports have her as Carla McCoy.

There's a set of nesting bowls—three—in a pumpkin-colored glaze. *You were a fall baby.* In the bottom of each, there's a swirly, hand-painted man and woman together. Their forms are so entwined you can't distinguish one from the other. Each bowl's united couple is a little larger than the last, to fill the slightly bigger area for the swirl of bodies at the bottom. They're all unique. In one, you see more of the woman's hips, and in another, you see her long curly hair entwined around them both, locking them in an embrace. In the biggest bowl, their bodies bend away from each other, legs entwined, but upper torsos arcing out—trying to get free. They tell a story, and I want more. I look in every piece for more of the man and woman, the way her hair sometimes lassoes him down, the way their tight embrace can be seen as love or as entrapment. As prison. Three sets of bowls tell this story of the good and bad of love, and on the bottom of each, *C. Robichaux*, etched into the clay with something sharp—a knife tip? Some pottery tool I don't know about? C. Robichaux. Carla. The hairdresser, the potter. Carla, sober. Carla, mother of me.

I spy the corner of a sheet of paper with her handwriting on it, sticking out from under a big book called *Ceramics*.

It's regular notebook paper and the handwriting is almost identical to mine. I slide it out from under the thick, hardback book. It's dated at the top—June 9th —*just three days before...*

> Admit that you are powerless (one day at a time)
> Plan **WEDDING!** But first prove you can be sober for six months.
> Make amends to Tate (and so many others, but first to Tate)
> Paint the outside of studio (something bright – raspberry? Key lime?)
> ~~Buy a used kiln~~
> Call Tate. Be persistent, but be patient. Earn back her trust.
> ~~Airline reservations - Santa Fe/Kevin~~
> Introduce Kevin and Tate before wedding
> Plan something with Tate – a trip? – before the wedding
> Every single day, be grateful, and don't drink.

I read this like it's some artifact from an ancient civilization, like it's a clue to life on other planets. My name appears five times—six if you count the possessive pronoun *her*. The way the list is numbered, the way it contains super important, life-changing items next to small, insignificant errands, the parentheticals qualifying everything—it could easily have been my own list. The way she put something on the list that she'd obviously already done—the kiln—I mean look at all this stuff already fired. I've done that too—put something on a list solely because it's already done, cross it out right away, feel good about goals already accomplished. I fold it up to the size of a matchbook, this paper she touched three days before her last, and slide it deep into my front jeans pocket.

Earn back her trust. Be patient.

In the end I take three pieces: the angel mug; the middle-sized bowl from the nesting set—one where the braided male and female forms appear happily entwined; and a dinner plate—in the blue glaze, with brick on the back and rim. This leaves seven plates like it—an incomplete set, but Greta said I should have whatever I want. I like the idea of having a plate, a bowl, and a cup *that she made*. A mother's job, one of them, is to feed her young.

I put these items on towels, roll them up tight, tuck the towel corner into the cup's opening. This reminds me of Sawyer, with the towel, that day at the pool. I put them into my backpack carefully, arranged so the flat back of the plate will ride against my own back. I tug on the cord to cinch the pack, and clamp it shut.

Then, I get up onto the stool of the potter's wheel, and I sit where she sat.

People have always told me I look just like my mom. This was meant as a compliment—no one would disagree that she's beautiful—but it was also just a fact. When I stopped having her in my life, our physical resemblance made it harder to convince people I wanted no part of her. *But you look just like her!* Knowing I looked like her, which meant I was pretty like she was, made some parts of adolescence less painful. But to have everyone telling you how much you look like your mother when your mother is a drunk and sometimes, frankly, behaves like a whore—your resemblance becomes problematic. I could excise her from my life but I could not help the fact that people would forever comment how I was her spitting image. There's a photograph of her that circulated everywhere after the murder—in the newspapers, online—even now it's on posters all over town, advertising the benefit. And you could absolutely think she's a slightly older version of me. The older I get, the more this is true. Cutting off all my hair doesn't change it. I tried that once.

But now, sitting in this seat where she sat, my butt where hers was, where, by centering slab after hunk after mound of clay, she found her own balance, I *feel* our similarities. I feel my posture settle into hers, my hips adjust themselves, my arms and shoulders like hers, over the wheel, my hands craving the malleability of clay.

I experiment, turning the wheel, figuring out how to control the speed. I need to try to make something. Surely there's some clay around here. I find some in a big, bench-like storage chest. Inside is a box and inside that are two 25-pound bags of raw clay—one unopened, the other hardly used. The edges are hard and crusty. I use a spade-like tool to cut through the hard part. It's moist underneath. Pliable. The deeper I dig, the more wet-fresh it gets.

I lift it out, turn the whole rectangle on its side, revealing a place where the clay was cut in a big L shape—sliced down and across and then pressed back together. It's misshapen there, like a small pregnancy, but the seams of the cut have been smoothed over by something flat—maybe by the very same spade I'm holding. The thought of this implement in my palm having been in hers only days before she died makes it suddenly precious. I look around and think of all the other things in here she touched.

I'm not sure why I do what I do next, but instinct takes over. I go at the clay with my hands. I dig. I feel cool clay fill up the space under each fingernail. I hit something hard—an edge. My finger follows it around—maybe four inches long? I dig around it until there's enough to grab onto and wrestle forth.

A hoe.

Just the metal part, with a half-inch of wooden handle, sawed-off edge.

Knotted up at the curve, a tangle of hair, and what looks like the brick of that one glaze, but is actually dried blood.

It doesn't take any time at all to know what I know. The head of this hoe was hidden here in this clay by Arthur McCoy, the accused.

CHAPTER TWENTY-THREE:

HERE OR ANYWHERE

The fact of it suffocates me; I'm short of breath. I need to get out, go somewhere green where there's a surplus of air, somewhere I can scream and not be heard. Exhaust myself on a trail up a mountain that doesn't end. Run fast to some other world, where fathers do not kill mothers, where the dictionary does not contain the word "bludgeon."

I put the clay and the evidence back in the chest, turn out the lights, and lock the door. I don't leave the key where we're supposed to leave it; it's deep in the same pocket that holds my mom's to-do list.

I don't remember making the turns, stopping for the big intersections, gliding up my driveway—*home*—but now I'm walking to the back, leaning my bike against the carport, locking it to the post. My life is a movie I'm watching. There's a studio behind a house; this must be where the girl lives.

My cells quake with what I know. *He did this. He actually did this.* There's not one person I can call. No one I can tell this to. Greta, Kale, Swimmer Boy. My *father*—I came from that man. His DNA.

Remembering the breakables in my backpack, I unload them onto my unmade bed. The place is a mess. I am a mess. Again, the urge to scream. To have something loud and raw exit my body. To have my throat open up and produce flames. Tate, the dragon.

It's after four, not even two more hours of daylight left. I fill a water bottle and put it in the pack, along with a wind-breaker. I take my wallet with driver's license, my phone, a notebook, a pen, and the only orange from the bowl of fruit. Only a week ago, I'd taken pleasure in buying and arranging that fruit—taking all the little stickers off, making sure to spread the colors around—putting the orange next to an apple, next to an avocado, laying the bananas across the top so they wouldn't bruise. *I will never feel that way again.* Can never go back to not knowing.

I was thinking, as I arranged the bowl, about nutrition. My mom always said that there were good carbs and bad carbs and fruits were the good.

It's never a bright idea to start driving until you know where you're going, but I need motion, so I head toward Mopac Expressway. I rule out the Hike and Bike Trail around Town Lake because it's too crowded. Power walkers and dogs and babies in jogger strollers. Mothers trying to lose their pregnancy weight. *Mothers.* I can't go to Mt. Bonnell, because that's where Jasper and I used to stargaze and smooch. Talk about another life entirely. I don't even know that girl any-more. And I don't want to think about Jasper. I can't go out to Pedernales, because 1) I'm not positive how to get there; and 2) I don't want to mess up that memory of a picnic with a sweet boy. That whole thing is so screwed now. I'll never know what it's like to kiss him.

It hasn't escaped me that I took the car without asking.

But if ever there should be an exception to a rule, it's now. I head south. Mexico sounds nice.

Winter is visible out the windows. Without even opening them to the frigid air, you can tell—things are grey, square, boxed up and shut down. Even the debris on the roadside distinguishes itself as winter trash. Convenience store burrito wrappers, to-go coffee cups, hot chocolate packets. No more popsicle sticks, or flattened Ben & Jerry's pints. Dark comes earlier and the city seems ready for it.

Dusk has always been my least favorite time. My scariest. It's a time when you don't belong. Here or anywhere. Separated from people you love by miles, multiplied by the waning of light. You might as well be driving a highway in South Dakota for how far you feel from the familiar.

I want suddenly to be back at the Grand Canyon, to be one of those hotdoggers who gets too close to the edge, who scrambles past cautionary signs onto crumbling ledges. Fall into something deep and jagged and endless? Bring it on. Show me your rattlesnakes.

I decide to stop caring. If I don't care, then life can't hurt so bad. I unbuckle my seat belt. I could sail through a windshield. Never have to go to school and know that people know.

I swing onto Bee Caves. You could drive off the edge of this road. Curvy and sometimes without guardrails, inviting hills on either side, and in the springtime, wildflowers. No flowers now, but I remember one time when I was seven, we came out here to take a family photo in a field of bluebonnets. Lupine is their real name. State flower. My mother loves bluebonnets. *Loved.*

That memory brings me to another one—the Wild Basin Preserve, right near here. Truthfully, the only time I've been on the trails there, I was either in a stroller or riding piggy back on my dad. The last time I was definitely old enough to walk, four or five, but I was being lazy. Walking long distances on dirt trails is boring for a kid, unless you are somewhere like a zoo or an amusement park. This was before Greta taught me to enjoy just being out in a wild place, enjoying nature. Neither of my parents camped or did much outdoors. But my mother had a thing for this place, because she'd read something about it in the newspaper, and she got pumped up about the fact that it got its designation as a preserve due to the efforts of seven women. They lived nearby, wanted to keep the area from being developed, so they did all the fundraising and all the battling with the city and the county, and after many years, they got their way. My mother found them an inspiration. This was before the drinking. She went to a fundraiser they had and, briefly, became a volunteer. A couple of the magnificent seven started going to her for their haircuts and to hide the grey. Because she liked Wild Basin, it was my job to dislike it, or feign disinterest. But now it is precisely where I want to go. *Wild* is what I'm after. A place where I can let out this guttural scream. It will sound like someone's been murdered, bludgeoned even, but only the bats and the armadillos will hear.

CHAPTER TWENTY-FOUR:

ENDANGERED

This Wild Basin doesn't provide the convenient risks of the Grand Canyon—no places to hurl oneself deftly off a cliff. A glance at the info board near the parking lot tells me a few things: The black-capped vireos and the golden-cheeked warbler have been known to make their habitat here; I am to watch out for the Timber Rattlesnake and scorpions; and even if I were to do every single stretch of trail here, I couldn't consume more than three miles. It's going to take a lot more miles than that to get where I'm trying to go—the point of extinction. I quickly abandon the marked trail.

Greta would be pleased to know I purposely left my cell phone in the car. Yes, me, the cell phone promoter. Safety first and all that. Safety can kiss my ass. There's no one I want to talk to and no one whose call I'd answer. A bird sings out high in one tree and another responds with the same sound, from across the way. I wonder if it's the vireos or the warbler. I would like to be able to speak their language, to translate the urgency in their messages. Birds confirm the uselessness of phones. Human beings are idiots. Modern medicine has made it so that you can change your gender, but a species change is what I'd sign up for. Make me a bird or a baboon. The imperiled sea turtle, the warbler with cheeks of gold.

I weave through low brush and am grateful for my jeans. If I were in shorts, my legs would be a maze of scratches and gashes. I know rattlesnakes curl up at the base of brush, and under rock overhangs, and instead of giving them a wide berth, I walk close; I cuff my jeans and tempt the snakes with bare, bony ankles. *Come and get it*. I blast through the branches and briars and prickly pear without hesitation.

When I no longer have a clue where the parking lot is, I stop. Stand still. And scream. Then listen. When nobody answers me back, I scream again. I do this till my throat hurts and the screaming almost becomes comical. I collapse, let the tears come.

An ant crawling on my hand wakes me up. It is pretty damn dark. Without my phone, which serves as my watch, I can't say what time it is, but I figure I've got maybe twenty minutes of visibility left if I'm going to find the trail and get back to the car. What satisfied me earlier—to have gotten so far off trail as to not recognize one single thing—now has me feeling stupid. I mean, if I'd planned on spending the night out here, I would've at least brought a sleeping bag, a flashlight, and something more to eat than an orange. Remembering this makes me hungry, but I can't lose the time it would take to peel and eat, so I get up, brush off my butt, and start walking.

You don't notice degrees of light until you are finding your way in a fast-approaching dark. The sun is still just barely over the horizon, and that side of the sky is still blue-bright with it. My eyes adjust. I move as fast as I can without tripping over the branches that knot up just a few inches off the ground. I make my steps high and hard, so I won't trip over anything I can't see, and so if I step on a snake, it'll be forceful enough to stun him. I unroll my cuffs so my jeans touch the top of my Chuck Taylors.

The light fades quickly. One minute I can see a cactus in front of me; the next minute, one I didn't see to my left rakes gullies into my forearm, big enough to plant a row of corn. Immediately, blood rises to the surface of each slice. Immediately, it stings. The injury feels equally physical and emotional. "Ow," I say, as though there were someone to hear me, or care. As long as I'm talking to myself, I go ahead and say it: "I want my mom." I sit down, take off my shirt, wet the sleeve a little with my water bottle, and press the cool, wet cloth into the cuts. I do this a couple times till the bleeding stops. It's cold sitting here in just jeans and a bra, but there's something nice about wild air kissing skin. *Swimmer Boy, where are you now?* I stuff the damp shirt into my backpack and put the fleece on with no shirt under it. It's time to layer up, anyway. When it gets colder, I'll add my windbreaker.

Finding the trail seems more and more unlikely. I know I hiked mostly downhill, so I've been going up and up and up this one slope, but there's nothing resembling a path. Even if I did cross over the trail, I don't know if I'd recognize it in this ravenous dark, which is swallowing everything up.

Who knows how much time passes—an hour maybe? An eon? I keep moving, unsnagging my feet when they tangle in the low brush, ducking when, out of nowhere, there's a branch about to take out my head. The toe of my shoe hits a boulder mid-stride, and I pedal through air in slow motion. Then I'm down, fast, hands first, in a low bush. As far as falls go, this one is not so bad. My left hand got jabbed by something dry and sharp, but nothing's bleeding. My fleece caught on something on the way down, and there are leaves and twigs stuck to the fabric like Velcro. I rest there for a second, realizing how fast my breath is coming, how long I've been running only to get nowhere, how foolish my strategy has been. It's dark. It's *past* dark. I'm probably spending the night out here. I might as well be blindfolded.

It strikes me that I should pretend I *am* blindfolded. Or even blind. If I couldn't rely on sight at all, even if it were bright daylight out here, if I couldn't see, what would I do? I'd have to rely more on hearing, taste, touch and smell—senses blind people develop better than the rest of us.

I close my eyes. I stay still and listen: silence so loud it hums. I don't hear birds anymore. I don't hear traffic or horns or sirens or music. But I could swear there is a sound the vegetation makes. Almost a creaking, like I'm hearing it grow. I reach my hand into the branches I've landed on, and I know it's a Manzanita. Normally, I know this plant by its deep red bark, but now I sense this through the bark's smoothness. I *see* with fingertips. I adjust my butt to get more comfortable and then take in a big whiff of Wild Basin air—some combination of oak leaves and acorns and remembered rain. It smells like dirt tastes. Sticking out my tongue, I feel how seldom it sees the world outside my mouth. I wag it around a little, feeling the cold air against my 98.6.

After waking up my taste buds, I decide I might as well relax long enough to eat my orange.

Funny how you really don't need to see to do things you do all the time with your sense of sight. Keeping my eyes closed, it's easy to find the zipper on my backpack. To feel for the top of it, the seams, the two different zippers, and the pull-cord inside. To reach in and grab the only round thing, so unmistakably an orange. The texture like some foreign skin, the smell when I puncture the peel with my thumb, the little exhaust of air and droplets of moisture when I bend the peel back to an unfamiliar arch. The undeniable stickiness left on fingers. If I could see, I know there would be that sparkly, clear stuff, almost like scales from a fish, a film attached to the skin. I separate off a section and put it in my mouth. Who needs sight?

It's the best orange I've ever eaten. The first orange ever in the known world. Garden of Eden orange. Tantalizingly sweet and cold, glorious and forbidden.

Post-fruit break, I am not so scared anymore. The scariest thing to me since the murder was the fact that the murderer was still on the loose. Even though my mother's house is a good five miles from where I lived with my dad, I would imagine sometimes that the murderer would come back for me, her lookalike. It wasn't rational, but neither was her murder. I remember an article in the paper, right after it happened, right after they took my dad in, that said residents of that neighborhood were worried, wanted police protection, wanted reassurance that it was safe for their children to play outside. The article quoted a policeman saying that people had nothing to worry about. That they should go about their business. The crime was one of passion, not a random individual coming through town to kill people. This was a one-time deal, a private matter, domestic violence. And he repeated: "What we're seeing here is a crime of passion." They'd convinced themselves my dad was the perpetrator, and now I know they were right.

Even with the knowledge of what he did, I'm not afraid of my father in the least. He wouldn't hurt a hair on my head. I'm his baby girl. And I no longer need to be afraid of the random man who did this to my mother because he wasn't, in fact, random. Even though I'm lost right now, don't have a clue which way to go to find the trail, I am not afraid. I *was* afraid, petrified—until I fell. You hear people say how you're more likely to get into a car accident two blocks from home than you are on the interstate. And it's about as likely that you'll be attacked by a grizzly as it is that you'd be struck by lightning, meaning *not very*. Or there's more of a chance that you'll get hurt or robbed or raped in the city than you will out in the middle of some wilderness. Sure, there are psychopaths and maniacs in the world, but my chance of meeting one out here in Wild Basin is about the same as my chance of shaking the hand of Bigfoot. If this were a movie, scary shit might happen. Girl gets lost in the woods and gnarly, crazy dude with a hook for a hand creeps up on her from behind, his arm covering her mouth so she can't scream, and carries her back to his underground shelter, where all manner of torture will ensue.

But this is no movie. This is just my ruined life.

So-called.

A cool thing I learned from the signs where I parked: the black-capped vireo is a migratory songbird with a repertoire of 1,700 different notes. The Wild Basin is participating in an effort to restore their habitat, which involves manipulating the vegetation back to the way those birds like it. Black-capped vireos are endangered, yet they sing.

CHAPTER TWENTY-FIVE:

BENEVOLENCE

1,700 notes is nothing to sneeze at. I would like to make this bird's acquaintance. The only things flitting around right now are bats. Talk about another instance when sight doesn't matter—bats do everything through some inner radar. Know when to swoop up or down, right or left, know how not to run into things. I close my eyes again, to see what I can hear. Smell, taste, touch.

I feel the twigs and small stones under my butt, and in between them, the softer surface. I take in a smell that is different, even, from a few minutes ago: it smells like dark, like the inside of a pecan shell. My ears pick up something new—a trickling? It's so faint, I can't be sure it's real. Comes and goes. But then it's steady long enough to make me believe in it. Something not far from here is dripping or flowing. Greta told me if you are ever lost in the wilderness, find a water source and follow it. If you're following a creek or stream or river, there's no chance of circling back on your own steps. The creek travels and by following it, you are likely to get somewhere new. I try to point to where the noise is coming from. I stand up, brush off, loop my arms through my back-pack. With eyes still closed, I head in its direction. I stumble and open my eyes. But it's true, I can't hear the water as well when sight competes with hearing. So I close them again and continue. Each time I question if I've gone in the right direction, I stop, listen, locate the sound again.

It's easier and easier to hear, and soon I open my eyes. I feel it, in the air, moisture. In the dark, I can't see it till I'm right on it; two more steps, and I would've dunked my shoe. *A creek. Something to follow.*

Left or right, I figure it doesn't matter. Either way will get me somewhere. I make a left, and, not three minutes later, as I'm skirting alongside this creek, there's a sudden light, and then my shadow, and I turn. Damn if it isn't a lopsided moon showing up to illuminate my way. The world's biggest flashlight. Between the moon and the creek, it's no time at all before I intersect with a trail. A trail! And on that trail is a bench. A bench! I might as well have discovered signs of an ancient civilization. Yes, people exist.

Why have I never gone hiking in moonlight before? I want to do this with Kale, with Greta. But mostly with Sawyer. For all the hours I've been lost, you would think I'd be tired, but this moonlit scene energizes me. I could keep this up forever.

At a trail intersection, there are signs. The creek is "Bee Creek." The trails are "Creek Trail" and "Falls Trail," and there's a sign with an arrow pointing the way to the Education Center, to the parking lot.

As I walk, I'm reminded of a story we read in Bower's class. "Walking Out" it was called, by a guy named David Quammen. One of the essay questions we could write about asked us to comment on how the author indicates that the natural world was indifferent to the suffering of the point-of-view character. That character was a boy whose father took him on a hunting trip in winter in Montana—to make a man out of him. Things got all messed up when they encountered a bear cub and her angry momma. In the ensuing mayhem, after the boy nearly loses his hand to the cub's teeth, his father helps him climb a tree and passes him the gun in case the bear comes climbing up after him. With a mangled hand, and dangling by his good arm from where he is in the tree, the boy does his best, but as he's receiving the gun, barrel down, he accidentally pulls the trigger, hitting his father below. The father is losing a lot of blood, and the boy has to take charge in an effort to save his father's life. Has to do all the things his father had done before: find food, make a fire, keep them both from freezing to death in this blizzard.

Toward the end, you get the sense that the father isn't alive anymore, but the son can't acknowledge this or he will lose his resolve, so he holds his father over his shoulder, and just keeps walking, in snow that is sometimes knee-deep. His progress is slow. Throughout it all, there's this backdrop of constant snow. And the author has lines like "The snow fell as gracefully as before," after something horrible has happened. The snow just falls, unfazed. I spent hours writing my essay on it. Bower's question said that nature was neither malevolent (bad) nor benevolent (good) as a force in the story. It was *indifferent*. And she asked us to find evidence for this in the text. How nature could not have cared less what was happening to the poor boy.

I wish I could tell Bower how the creek showed up, buoyant, right when I needed it, and how that alone would've been enough, but then nature, benevolent, offered up the moon.

CHAPTER TWENTY-SIX:

NOTHING BUT THE TRUTH

My car is the only one in the parking lot, and someone has left the gate open so I can drive out of here. The sign says the gate is only open from sunrise to sunset—someone was looking out for me. I check my phone, but just for the time. I'm not ready to read any texts or hear any voicemail. Midnight on the dot. Like some girl in a fairy tale, I've made it back just before the stroke of the clock that would turn this car back into a pumpkin. *The car.* Oops. I just may be in deep shit with Uncle Jim.

Being in the car, seeing the dash light up, makes it all real again. *How could he have done this?* Among the things I resent my father for is this information that I now have, me alone. The outcome of this case, his future, is in my hands. Now tell me if that sounds fair to you. Do I call the cops, turn over the head of the hoe? Do I wait and leave it to fate? See if they ever discover this evidence on their own? Do I destroy what I found? Remove all trace? Throw it deep into Lake Travis? Kill myself, and take this knowledge with me?

Let's face it: Tate McCoy is not going to commit suicide. Maybe I'm too solid. Maybe I'm too much of a weenie. I entertained the idea, I really did. I even wondered if there was such a thing as bludgeoning yourself, but I had a hard time envisioning it, even with my eyes closed.

There's comfort in knowing the truth, even when the truth is horrific. At least it's definite, inarguable now—he did it. I *am* that girl whose dad killed her mom.

Isn't this what I always wish for on *Dateline* and *48 Hours?* Resolution? I want answers, confessions, absolutes. I want to know, by the end of the show, did the guy poison his wife or did he not? Was it the lover the woman had on the side or her husband who strangled her? Was it the husband who shot his wife, or was it a suicide as he claims? But in the end, most of the time, all you can hope to learn is whether he was found guilty or not guilty. There's no guaranteed relationship between that and the *truth.* This has been hard for me to swallow. That our so-called justice system is a game of power, of who can afford what fancy lawyer. It's like the lawyers for the defense don't concern themselves with whether he did it or not. What matters is if they can get him off. When I watch these shows, I get crazy mad. What I want to know is *did he do it*? You learn the *outcome,* which does not necessarily have any relationship to the truth. Whatever happened to the truth? I want God to come down and point a finger: It was him! Over there! The bearded bartender she was dating! I want clarity and certainty and those shows rarely provide it. I want the whole truth and nothing but the truth, and now I have it. So help me, God.

CHAPTER TWENTY-SEVEN:

YES AND NO

On the way home, I go through the late-night drive-through for some tacos. Avocado and lettuce and tomato. I'm starving. I try out my plan against different backdrops—the Wild Basin parking lot, Bee Caves Road, and now a Mexican fast food place—in all of these locations, the answer is the same: I have to tell.

I scarf down the food and wish I'd ordered four tacos instead of three. I wash it all down with pink lemonade. I drive home, turning off the lights as I near the driveway, not wanting to risk waking Uncle Jim. *Uncle Jim, the relatives, everyone will soon know.* I park and creep to the back, let myself in. Things look both the same and different. It's my place, my mess, my dirty clothes on the floor, but I am not the same girl as before. I peel off my clothes and crawl into bed, where I sleep the sleep of the dead.

I wake up and it hits me: *Did he do it? Or was that just a bad dream?*

I face my phone, which I couldn't do last night. Strings of messages from the usual suspects. Everybody wants to know where the hell I've been. And two from Jim. 1) He wants to know why I took the car without asking; and 2) he wants to have a discussion about my refusal to observe curfew. What consequence do I think would be appropriate?

What consequence, Uncle Jimmy? I'm pretty sure I've been dealt plenty of those.

I don't call anyone back. Knowing what I know is one thing; sharing it is another. I prepare for a surprise visit from Uncle Jim, which means I have to clean the studio. As messy as I am, once I get into it, I enjoy cleaning. It's one of those mindless activities that allows you to meditate on things, and that's what I do, most of the afternoon.

Between the vacuuming and the dishes, I come up with a plan that's got some compromise in it. I have to turn this evidence over to the police, I know this. But I want to tell my father first, give him the opportunity to come clean. The thought of seeing him makes my stomach want to surrender its lunch. All afternoon, I procrastinate. Before leaving, I put a note on the door of the big house. *Taking the car, but I'll be back early. Sorry if I worried you last night.*

This pre-dusk drive is different from last night's. I vacillate between shock over what I've discovered, and shock that I'm *not* in shock. If there was even one ounce of me that thought I might be wrong, that the murder weapon was put there by a different man than my father, I'd be heading to the jail with a measure of hope.

He saved the handle of the hoe. Thought it might one day be useful, serve a purpose. What brand of crazy lets you have this thought after murdering your ex-wife? These thoughts, combined with encroaching dark, creep me out. The whole Play-Doh game? That memory is forever ruined.

Christmas lights come on at several houses, making those of us outside feel lonelier. How late is too late to leave your lights up after Christmas? My mother always said they had to come down by the 6th of January. I have no idea why that was the arbitrary day. Today is the 7th. The 6th was the day I learned the impossible about my father.

There is never total privacy during our visits; a guard is always within earshot. I don't want anyone but my father to hear what I have to say. This isn't some *48 Hours* moment. I don't have a plan. I don't even want to see him. But I keep driving because I've procrastinated so long that there are only twenty-two minutes left of visiting time. I need to give him a chance to come clean before this comes out in the papers.

The guard is Eula, one of my favorites. She treats me like I'm normal.

"Hey, sugah," she says. "How was your Christmas?"

I tell her fine, it was fine. I try to act like this is any old visit. "I know I'm late," I say.

"Well honey," she says, "between you and me, I don't care about the time. I'm here and you're here and you want to see your father. You go on in and take your time. Nobody's gonna know if you're here past hours except me and I say it's okay." She takes the big ring of keys and goes to get my father. "It's the holidays," she adds. I hear her put him in a room. I hear her say "It's Tate." I hear her walking back toward me.

She lets me into the room he's in, and for a moment I feel like begging her to stay. *Help me do this.* But I just smile at her and say thanks. And then she walks away, like really away. Like completely out of earshot. Like this is her Christmas gift to us.

If my father knows me even half as well as I think I know him, if we ever had a telepathic connection, he should be able to tell on sight that there is something horribly wrong.

What he says is, "This is an unexpected surprise."

I just look at him.

"What is it, honey?"

"Guess," I say.

He shakes his head. "Are you sick? Did someone hurt you?"

I nod. That would most definitely be a yes.

Dad says, "Is this about the house? Uncle Jimmy?"

"Dad," I say, my own voice sounding foreign, "I know."

He registers what I've said, and his face shifts to reclaim the stance, the expression, of innocence. He's practiced this look. He's good at it, and it comes back, but it's the brief look I witness before that tells me I'm right.

"I found the hoe. The head of it in the clay. I know it was you."

The expected charade begins. *He doesn't know what I'm talking about; start all over at the beginning and tell me what happened; it's clear you're upset, honey; I want to help.*

"Dad! Don't do this! You can lie all you want to the lawyers and the judge and the jury, but I'm asking you right now, right here, as your *daughter*, to not lie to me. I mean come on, Dad. The Play-Doh game."

He's quiet, which is preferable to the verbal scramble.

"I'm telling you," I say, "that whether you come clean or not, *I know*. And I can turn in the evidence tomorrow, with or without a confession. But I know. And this is the last time you're ever going to see me, so if you have something to say to me, now's the time."

My father, Arthur McCoy, the accused, fiddles with the hem of his uniform shirt. He shrinks there in front of me—a suddenly small man, stooped.

"I can't expect you to understand," he says.

I'm quiet, waiting. I focus on the dust curled around the foot of the table leg, like that hair wrapped at the bend in the hoe, holding on.

"You're too young to understand," he tries.

I don't dignify that with any response.

"You have no idea," he says. "I needed her to not exist anymore."

The statement, the damning sentence, flits around the small room for a second, circling the light fixture, floating up and then down, landing in front of me on the table. *To not exist.*

"You disgust me."

He makes the same stop sign gesture his brother uses. "Tate," he says.

"All the bad stuff Mom did in her life, is nothing compared to this."

"Tate," he says. "I only ever loved her. I still love her. She was the love of my life."

Part of me listens and another part of me watches myself in this moment. *Pay attention*, that part says. *This is a pivotal moment in your life.*

He could live with the failure of their marriage as long as he saw that failure as a result of her problem—addiction—as long as he saw her like one of his more hopeless patients. When she reinvented herself for another man, cleaned up her act but still had no use for him, it all came back. The lying, the cheating, the drinking, and he felt she did not deserve one moment of her newfound happiness, since she'd robbed him of his dreams with her. It was the news of her engagement that sent him over the edge. *How dare she?*

I ask him if he's finished. He says, "For now, yes, sure." His calm demeanor makes me think of horror movies, of *The Shining*, a calm that seems to accompany insanity.

"I just want to know, did you think about me at all?"

He appears to ponder this.

"I lost Mom because of you. I lost anything resembling a normal life this last year and a half. I lost Maddie, my little sister. I'm losing the studio, and maybe my friends if I have to do my senior year somewhere else."

It's like he's wearing some protective glaze. Nothing I say gets through the gloss.

"Are you going to tell them, or should I?"

"Tell them?" he says.

"Change your plea to guilty."

"Tate, this legal thing is like a game—a very sophisticated game. We can win this one. The prosecution has done a very poor job. All the jury has to be convinced of is reasonable doubt. That thing you found, that weapon, there's nothing definitively linking that to me."

"*Me*, Dad. I'm the link."

"Well, that's your decision, Tate. If you wish to testify and share the content of this conversation, that's up to you. But I would urge you to think really hard about how much more you stand to lose if I'm convicted."

"Dad, what has *happened* to you? You'd continue to lie about this? You've preached honesty to me my whole life. "

He doesn't say anything—which is good, because I'm not finished. I get up from the table, ready to make my final exit. My chair makes a discordant sound as it scrapes the concrete floor. If this were a movie, it's the exact sound effect they would want for this moment. A bleat. A cry. A sympathy conjured between inanimate surfaces. Sometimes I would like to push the mute button on the world.

"I'm surprised that after you killed her you didn't kill yourself. I don't know how you can live one day, one hour, with the knowledge of what you've done."

I start to leave, but turn back toward him. "And seriously, Dad, a *hoe*? Is that supposed to be some sort of really bad pun?"

Arthur McCoy, speechless.

"I guess I'm too young to understand," I say, and leave, without turning back.

I ring the bell for Eula to come get me, to walk me through all the locked corridors and release me to the January world outside.

She's holding her place in *People* magazine when she rounds the corner with all her keys.

"Already?" she says.

I nod.

"You can stay longer, sugah, if you want."

"We're done," I say, and I try to smile. I say thanks as she lets me out to the darkening night.

"Happy New Year, ya hear?" she says, and that's when the crying starts.

I drive to my mom's, open the studio door with the key I've kept, walk to the storage chest, lift the lid, just to be sure it's still there. *Like where would it have gone?* I call Sawyer.

It's been three weeks since we've spoken—I've been ignoring his messages and emails, the nice Happy New Year card he sent. He answers immediately. "Tate?" he says, and all I say is "I need your help." I tell him the address.

He says, "Are you okay?"

"Yes and no," I say. "Just hurry."

I think about what I'll say and how I'll say it. Sure, this could be the last time I ever see him; he could decide my life has become a little too sordid; but I'm suddenly ready for answers.

When his lights show up in the driveway, out by the for sale sign, I stand up. I practice again in my head what I'm going to say. Sometimes boys have a way of taking over, even when you don't want them to; they can tell you what to do or how to think. Sawyer's not like that, really, but this is too important a moment to be passive while someone else decides the course of action. I've done my thinking. I've already decided what to do. I just want a friend here while I'm doing it.

Sawyer comes toward the back and when he sees me standing inside my mother's pottery studio, he smiles a swimmer-boy smile. It's been too long since I saw that.

I open the door, and he comes in. We hug. His face is a big question mark.

I go over to the chest and he follows. I lift the lid so he can see it there—the sawed-off handle, the dried blood, the tangle of my mother's hair.

"I need to call the police and turn this in, and give a statement," I say. "And I need you here with me while I do it."

CHAPTER TWENTY-EIGHT:

GENUINE LOVE

Two days later, Sawyer calls, late afternoon, says he has to see me. I'm at my job at Big Brothers Big Sisters. I ask Mags if I can take a break—I'm pricing donated clothes for the thrift shop, folding and sorting them. She says sure, take fifteen minutes, so I wait for Sawyer outside. I sit on the curb, close my eyes, and try to think of something, anything, besides what it will be like that first time we kiss. I know now that we've made up, it's going to happen and it's going to be soon. You would think that, given the events of the last couple of days, I wouldn't be stuck in my head on swimmer-boy fantasies. There's a lot of room in one brain, I guess, for a variety of thoughts. I hear a car and open my eyes.

He heard it from his journalism teacher who heard it from his wife who heard it on the car radio during her lunch hour: Arthur McCoy confessed to the murder of his wife. Word is spreading fast and Sawyer didn't want me to hear it from anyone but him.

Two days ago a homicide detective met us at the pottery studio and took us and the evidence—clay and all—back to the station. I gave a statement. I told the truth.

We don't know if Arthur's confession came out of the knowledge that they had the murder weapon and my statement. We don't know when the lawyers for the defense and the prosecution would've been notified. Wheels turn slowly and it could've been a couple of weeks before this new development would have been admissible. We don't know what sort of pressure he was under and I'm okay with not knowing. Did he confess because he felt he had no choice? Did he confess because he wanted, finally, to stop the charade?

Not five minutes after Sawyer pulls into the parking lot, here comes the gold Prius, the TV reporter with her handheld camera. For the first time, I don't even care. Let her ask me whatever she wants; I've got nothing to hide. And if it was my McCoy family pride that kept me from giving her the time of day, well, that's gone, evaporated.

Sawyer starts to get up and tell her to get lost, but I say, "It's okay." The whole city is finding out the truth. The newspaper will have it, probably front page, in the morning. People are calling and emailing and texting each other: *Did you hear?* I've got Sawyer with me. I've got maybe three minutes left of this break from my job and if the *Dateline* reporter wants to talk to me, so be it.

She starts with what she always says: her name (Pauline), the name of the show (*Dateline*), and the line "If I could just have a few minutes of your time…" I notice she's switched to more sensible shoes.

I look at my watch. I tell her I'm on a break from work, but she can have three minutes.

"You've heard about your father's confession?" she says.

"Yes."

"It must be devastating for you."

"I've known," I tell her, "for a few days."

"So he told you first?"

Mags bursts through the door, clapping her hands, like she's breaking up a dog fight or something.

"Go on," she says to the reporter. "Tate's working right now." She puts an arm around me and leads me inside.

Pauline shifts her focus to Sawyer.

"Did Arthur McCoy confess to his daughter before confessing in the courtroom?" she says. She's dying to get this info before anyone else.

Reporter Boy says, "It's more complicated than that."

Pauline follows him as he walks away. "Are you Tate's boyfriend?" she says, and my sense of hearing is suddenly heightened. *What will one-who-swims say?*

"Workin' on it," he says. "You can quote me on that."

Mags gives me a wink, and Sawyer takes the other side of me, and the three of us walk in. Mags says, "I just heard, honey. I'm so sorry." The two of them hug me into a huddle of genuine love.

CHAPTER TWENTY-NINE:

A Place to Start

Greta and Meg have already paid for their flights, but they think we should postpone the benefit, given the timing. Or, they say, they can do it without me, but I actually want to be there. Then we'll reschedule, Greta says, but I convince her it's okay, *I'm* okay. We decide to keep it as is. Advertising has gone out; posters are up around town; wine's bought and a caterer is reserved.

On the one hand, now that his guilt is out there, I worry this event will bring the nosiest people on the planet out of their homes. It'll be a showcase for my so-called ruined life. Come see the girl who lived to tell about it! The Fat Lady, The Thin Man, The Two-Headed Baby, our very own freak show with me at the center. But I feel strangely calm. We've got certainty now. Absolutes. And it's at least a place to start—here are the facts—now move on.

Greta and Meg insist on taking me out shopping for a dress. The benefit is a dress-up affair, and they don't think what I've planned to wear is snazzy enough. We end up in and out of stores at the mall, hours in fitting rooms—not my favorite thing—but finally we find the perfect dress. It's the midnight blue of my mother's favorite pottery glaze. It's strapless. It's stunning. It's expensive.

Greta says she doesn't care. It's a special occasion. We're remembering Carla. I tell her I will wear it again. I will use it for prom. "Tate, it's okay. You're lovely in it, and it's worth every penny." There's the fact of it being strapless and this being January. Meg finds a cropped sweater—a delicate mohair—a blue and brown weave. "That's it," Greta says. "That's the one."

At the cash register, while Meg rifles through a rack of sale stuff, Greta pulls out her credit card, and I notice she's crying. I don't want to say anything in front of the saleslady, who likely knows exactly who we are. But as soon as we step away, I look and confirm that Greta has remnants of tears in her eyes.

"Garbo?" I say.

She shakes her head.

"It's just you...in that dress," she says. "And how your mom won't get to see you...and how you look exactly like her."

I saw this myself, in the fitting room mirror. Dressed fancy, the resemblance was even more noticeable. And it doesn't bother me anymore. In fact, it's kind of cool.

I stop, right there in the aisle, and give my Aunt Greta a big hug.

"I miss her," she says. She sniffs.

"I miss her, too," I say, and it's the first time I've said it out loud.

CHAPTER THIRTY:

WoW

A local gallery has donated the space for the benefit, and the place is packed. People are unbelievably generous. Some aren't even leaving with a piece of my mother's work ("a Robichaux" they are now calling it, like suddenly it's a household word) but are just writing out donation checks. As the beneficiary of this benefit, I help Greta greet people, I smile, I thank them for coming out to remember my mom and to see her work.

Sure, some of them give me looks that I interpret as surprise—that I'm here, that I'm dressed up, that I'm not a basket case in a hospital gown in some mental ward. Some people came to see what they could see, but most of the people are nice, sincere. No one asks nosy questions. Pauline from *Dateline* is in the room, and even she leaves me alone. Meg made her leave her camera in the car. She buys a set of nesting bowls with the bodies painted in the bottom.

The Finches show up (Jasper's mom and dad), and our neighbors, the ones on both sides and the ones from across the street. There are two teachers from our school—Bower and the guy who teaches journalism. Mags is here, and two other people I work with at Big Brothers. Not one person from my father's side of the family shows up. There are a gazillion people I don't recognize. I guess all the publicity the case has received is finally, on this night, a positive.

Kale, Simon, and Sawyer are servers, carting around appetizers on trays. Kale has on a smokin' hot mini-skirt, a sweater, and faux-leather boots. She's a vegan who doesn't eat *or wear* animal products. She looks great. Simon let Sawyer wear some of his clothes and he's all dapper. A pin-striped button-down, ironed and crisp. Black pants (that butt!) and a bright blue tie. The only thing wrong with his outfit is the shoes—trail runners. He manages to swing by me more often than Kale or Simon do—making sure I get my share of bruschetta, candied pecans, tiny tacos, and itty bitty quiche. I'm eating everything without even thinking about whether there is cheese or eggs or butter or milk.

"Kale," I say, when she gets within shouting distance. She comes over. "Top of the evenin', Leafy Green."

"And sincerest of salutations to you."

"Hey," I say. "I need to confess on the vegan thing. I'm blowing it. I think I'm quitting. Officially. Tonight."

"That's okay, Tater."

"I think I need to try it some other time when I understand better all the reasons to do it."

"That makes total sense," she says. "I mean, really, you've had a few things going on in your life of late. Just a few. You should just eat whatever the hell you want."

"Did you see Jasper's parents?"

"I did. What is that tent his mother is wearing? I mean I know they are Quakers, but someone should call the fashion police. Did you see Her Royal Highness, Ms. Bower?"

"Roger that. She bought something, too."

"Oh my. Who is that guy?" Kale motions toward a movie-star-looking man in a corduroy jacket the same color as my dress. He's been staring at me since he arrived.

"No clue," I say. "But you should go see if the lad is hungry."

"The lad," she says. "The bloke... hold this for a sec." She hands me her tray while she straightens her skirt and tugs on her tights. "There are large amounts of cash floating around this place, Tater," she says.

"I know."

"I found something I want," she says. "Those little salt and pepper bowls with the tiny spoons? I'm buying one of those."

"You don't have to buy it, Kale. You can have it, for helping. Really."

Without responding, she heads away from me, so smoothly she might as well be on skates. She goes toward the dashing fellow, who is twice our age, at least. He looks over at me. I watch him turn down Kale's food offer, and now that I'm solo, he walks toward me. I busy myself with a price card that won't stay standing. I refold it, perch it next to the large vase.

I hear him before I see him.

"You look so much like Carla, I'm stunned."

I turn. I smile. I hold out my hand. "Tate," I say.

He says, "Obviously."

"Thanks so much for coming."

"I was engaged to marry your mother," he says.

I take this in. *So this is Kevin.*

"She was the love of my life," he adds.

"Well," is all I can come up with.

"Well," he says. "Indeed."

"Nice to meet you," I add.

Sawyer has been glancing over at us, and approaches

with his tray of truffles, right as Mr. Dapper hands me one of his business cards.

Sawyer's expression, as Mr. Dapper walks away, is classic.

"Hey," I say. "You look terrific."

Sawyer says, "Ahem. *You* do. Grown men are falling all over themselves to give you their business cards."

"That's the guy. The one my mother was going to marry."

"And now he wants to marry you, her look-alike."

I punch him and he almost loses the tray. Several truffles hit the floor.

"Sorry!" I pick them up.

"Three second rule?" he says, holding out the tray in case I want to put them back.

I think about it, then shake my head.

"Event's too classy for the three second rule." I toss them in a trash can.

"Your Aunt Meg is cool. She's sneaking me wine in those paper cups that are for the kids' punch."

"Oh," I say. "Well let's just mosey on over there and get some punch, then. If I've ever been ready to indulge, tonight would be the night."

I go over to where Meg is pouring and selling wine.

"I hear the *punch* is delightful," I say to her, giving the word punch the necessary punch so she knows what I'm after.

"Yes," she says. "Very good punch tonight." She pours me half of a little Dixie cup of red.

"Can I get some for Kale and Simon?"

She pours me a couple more.

Sawyer picks up a cup and holds it out to her.

"I'm cutting you off," she says. "He's had two already."

"They're miniscule!" I say.

"And he's driving my niece home tonight, so the answer is no."

Sawyer puts the tray of truffles down, since the evening appears to be coming to a close. A few people mill about. There is almost no merchandise left. A couple of mugs, a vase, two mismatched plates. We go off to deliver the wine.

"I'm driving you home?" Sawyer says.

"I don't know. Did you say that to Meg?"

"I didn't say anything."

"So Meg's playing Cupid."

"Something like that."

"Or she's just reading my mind."

"Yeah?" says Sawyer. "You were thinking that?"

"I'd love it if you'd drive me home."

"Hot damn," Sawyer says.

This is a very un-Sawyer-like exclamation. I laugh.

"What's happened to you, one-who-swims?"

"I don't know," he says. "Heartbreak? Bubonic Plague? I was afraid we might not ever be together."

"It was stupid. It was my fault, the whole thing. What you were saying was true, I just couldn't hear it."

"I'm sorry," Sawyer says. "In case I haven't officially said that yet."

"You said it a bunch. I'm sorry, too."

If I weren't standing here holding two tiny cups of vino, I would throw my arms around this boy's neck.

"Yo, Leafy!" I say, and Kale turns.

"A little adult beverage for you and the beau."

"Cheers," she says, and thuds soggy cups with Simon before they drink.

"That's kind of yummy," Kale says, "but I don't drink."

"It's vegan," I tell her. "It's grapes."

We stick around long enough to help clean up, but then

Meg and Greta tell the four of us to get lost. It's a Saturday night. We should go be teenagers. We all walk out to the parking lot together. The night is icy for Austin. The sky couldn't be more clear.

Kale dances around, trying to stay warm in her miniature outfit. "What should we do?"

I give her a look. My intriguing, sexy look. It's a look she's given me when she needed me to scram.

"Oh," Kale says, "really? Say no more, you hot po-Tate-er, you."

I punch her.

"Ow," she says.

Sawyer says, "You're abusing people a lot tonight. She hit me, too."

Simon says, "It's in her genes."

I'm not gonna lie. It stings.

Kale punches Simon. "THAT," she says, "IS NOT FUNNY."

Simon says sorry. Then he says, "Hey, I'm *really* sorry."

"It's okay. I mean, you're right about the genes."

"Yeah," Kale says, "but you are never going to be that..."

I nod, and get a hug from Kale and Simon. Kale says, "Ta-ta, and regards to the fam."

They head one way and we go the other, toward Sawyer's car. "It's over here," he says, and puts his arm around me. "I don't know about you, but January just became my favorite month."

We can't even wait till we get to my place. He leans over right there in the car. Kissing him is like the first slice of orange I ate in the total darkness of Wild Basin, eyes closed, all other senses heightened. Sweet and glorious and a tiny bit forbidden. I've never waited quite so long for something I wanted so badly. Every part of my body wakes up.

"Wow," I say.

"I know," he says.

"Don't stop," I say, and he doesn't.

CHAPTER THIRTY-ONE:

A CINDERELLA NIGHT

Hours dissolve in kissing bliss and eventually, the fancy clothes come off, bundled in a pile on the floor. I'm in a bra and underwear, no different from the swimsuit he's seen me in plenty of times. He's in his boxers, no different from his swimsuit, either. It's fitting, somehow, that we look to be dressed for Barton Springs, where it all began.

It's kind of amazing when you think about it, how many hours you can lie with someone, kissing him, and not get tired of it. Kissing like this, after so much anticipation, is like some kind of time travel. Not unlike swimming long distance. Like buoyancy. Every now and then we come back to Earth, to Austin, to this studio, this sofa, and we look at each other and smile, or sometimes laugh. Then we dive back down to that place of balance, just below the surface.

Sawyer's phone goes off—we ignore it but it rings again, and five minutes later, again. We dig through the clothes on the floor to find his pants, the phone in the pocket. It was his parents. Of course it was.

"Shit," he says. "It's two in the morning!"

Sawyer calls them right back.

"Mom," he says. "Sorry. I forgot to call."

I can hear his mom ranting a bit. Sawyer holds the phone away from his ear, rolls his eyes at me.

"I know," he says. "I'm sorry. I wasn't keeping track of the time."

I go to the sink and get some water.

"I'm at Tate's. No, her two aunts are here, too. Mom. Put Dad on the phone." He rolls his eyes again. I can't believe he's standing here, in my studio, in his boxers, in the middle of the night!

"Hey, Dad. Listen, I'm going to stay over here at Tate's house. Her aunts are here, and they are okay with it. It's too late to come home now. We fell asleep."

It's the only part that's a lie.

"Okay." Then, to me, "He's talking it over with my mom."

"Dad, tell her I'm sorry. I'll be home in the morning."

He puts his arms around me.

"I guess I should have asked you first. Can I stay over?"

"They were okay with it?"

"No. Actually, he said be home in twenty minutes or you're grounded."

"You should go then!"

"I'll go in the morning."

"But you'll be grounded."

"There's a first time for everything." I laugh.

"Yeah, I've never been grounded, either."

"That makes us well-matched," he says. "I promise I will tell you what it's like."

"Here," I say, "Put these on." They are some baggy boy's sweat pants of mine that should fit him fine. I get some PJs and brush my teeth and we pull back the covers and get in.

Sawyer says, "So I've wanted to ask you something." He

pauses. "You're beautiful, obviously, but it seems like you don't know it, or don't believe it, or you don't care, or you don't want to be pretty, I don't know. I'm just curious. Most girls who look like you, well, they know it. But the way you look doesn't faze you."

I tell him what Greta always told me: Beauty isn't something you can take personal credit for. Beauty is God-given, not something you've achieved or worked for. It's pretty much irrelevant, and if you treat it that way, it'll never work against you. Don't play it up, don't use it to manipulate anyone, and don't think that being pretty is the be all and end all. So you're pretty. Big deal. What are you going to do with your life? My mother was pretty, but it wasn't till she decided to be something other than pretty that she got a life worth living.

Sawyer nods. "Yet another thing that makes you so cool."

"Come here," I say.

For a short time, I let myself bask in the sweetness of this night—the fancy dress, meeting the man who would've been my step-dad, the generosity of the people who bought things and gave money, and then Sawyer at the end of it all, like the grand prize. It's a Cinderella night, like I tried on the glass slipper and it fit and now I've got the prince. But then a bad feeling moves in, the stark reality of what this night meant. What is my father doing right now? Sleeping? Thinking? Wishing he were dead?

"You asleep?"

Sawyer says no.

"You know what I wonder?"

Sawyer says what.

"Why was that Kevin guy never a suspect?"

"Well, he probably would've been. But he had an alibi. He doesn't even live here, so I'm sure he was able to prove he was in New Mexico when this happened."

"He says she was the love of his life. It's sad how they fell in love and it was all so brief."

"Okay, here's what's keeping me awake," Sawyer says. "Why do you think your dad left that hoe in the clay in the studio? It's kind of a miracle the homicide detectives didn't confiscate everything suspicious from the house and the studio, and search it. Seems like your dad would've expected that, and gotten rid of it."

"He actually told me. I didn't want to hear it at the time, but the night I confronted him, he told me all these details. He planned to go back. He was going to turn it into a pot of some kind, a big vase or something, and then he was going to glaze it and fire it in the kiln. He was going to put it in his house, on the mantle. But they came for him more quickly than he thought, and he never got to finish."

"That would've been a heavy vase."

"It's a strange idea," I say. "On the shows, people usually hurl the murder weapon into a river or a lake or the ocean. Never have I heard of someone hiding it in clay."

I think about sharing with Sawyer the detail of the Play-Doh game, but there's a sweetness to the memory—a toy dinosaur buried in clay; years later, the key to my studio. Talking about it, I don't know, might just be too sad.

I'm so close to sleep, I almost cannot summon the energy to speak.

"Goodnight," I say, almost a whisper.

But Swimmer Boy is already there.

I wake the next morning to see Greta peering through the window. I watch her as her eyes adjust, survey the room, see clothes on the floor, two people in the bed, the bare shoulders of Swimmer Boy next to me, lying on his side. Then she sees that I'm awake. I smile. I do a tiny pinky wave.

Greta opens her mouth wide, like dentist-wide, and gives me a thumbs-up.

She disappears for a minute, then comes back with a big piece of paper, which she holds up flat against the window. Written on it in black magic marker is this: **$26,000.** I lift my head a little, to be sure I'm seeing it right, to be sure of how many zeroes. It's my turn to open my mouth in shock. This is more than we ever expected to raise. I give Greta double thumbs-up. She pulls the paper down and writes something else on the back side, then puts it up against the glass again for me to read. It says, **HANG UP YOUR DRESS.**

CHAPTER THIRTY-TWO:

FAIRY GODFATHER

Turns out this *is* a Cinderella story and I have a fairy godfather: Kevin. That same day, he drops off an envelope. My name is on the outside. Inside is a letter, handwritten on both sides of a page, and a check made out to Tate McCoy for $100,000.00. At the bottom, where people put a note on what the check was for, he has written, GIFT.

Greta and I look at each other in shock.

"Holy shit," she says.

"Oh my God," I say. "Is he really rich or something?"

"He manages a bunch of real estate—but I had no idea he could write out a check like this."

I unfold the letter. He has nice handwriting. I read it out loud to Greta.

Dear Tate,

I apologize if I was at all intrusive last night at the benefit. Carla showed me pictures of you, but to see you in person, after losing her, the resemblance was just uncanny.

Your mother told me a good bit about your relationship—it concerned her a great deal. I don't know if you'd agree, but she was of the opinion that you and she were very close to reconciling. And she looked forward to that, I dare say, more than she looked forward to our wedding! Understandably. She'd known you a lot longer.

A brief history of our brief love: It was one of those divine coincidences. I'm in Santa Fe, but I was invited to be a guest speaker for a big AA meeting here in Austin. Carla was only one month sober at the time. I've got 20 years. It's against all the rules in AA for someone with that much sobriety to hook up with someone newly sober. The issues are very different—night and day. But I couldn't leave that meeting without at least making her acquaintance. We began corresponding by phone and email.

She came to see me, twice. And on the second visit, I asked her to marry me. This was one of those very rare moments of certainty life dishes up. I'm 44 years old, never even came close to marrying someone else. With Carla, I just knew. I saw no reason to wait. It wasn't like we were kids. She's the one who wanted to wait, to have more sobriety under her belt.

She was to fly in for a full week on the 15th of June. Her life was ended on the 12th. I thought mine ended that day as well. It has taken me a year to begin to imagine a life for myself without her.

One of the main things your mother wanted to do in her recovery was to make amends to you, to travel with you, to give you all the things she had not given you when she was consumed by drink. She wanted to get to know you all over again. She was proud of you, how you turned out, without much help from her as a mom. That was her biggest regret and what she most wanted to change.

Had we married, I would've been honored to become your step-father. Having given this a good bit of thought, and also having talked it over with your aunt, I can't see any reason why I can't still be like a step-father to you.

You will want to think about all this, and I know you don't know me and maybe don't even feel a need for another parent figure in your life. I've told your Aunt that you and she have an open invitation to visit me, should you find yourselves in Santa Fe. I would be happy to pay for the airfare and there is plenty of room at my house.

Meanwhile, please add this donation to the funds raised at last night's benefit. It seems it's the least I can do to help Carla, my beloved, achieve what she wanted most.

Respectfully,

Kevin Griffith

"I told you he was nice," Greta says.

"You knew about this?"

"Not about the check. But when we talked, he struck me as really sincere."

"What do you think he wants me to do with the money?"

"Well, I don't know what he's thinking, but I know what I'd do with it." If we add up his donation, the money raised at the benefit, the remaining insurance money, and a bit that Greta has saved, we can put a sizable down payment on the house, rent out the front, and put that rent toward a reasonable mortgage and upkeep. She says the house should even make us money on years where there are no big repairs.

I just about maul her. Greta says cease and desist.

"I love you," I say. "I will take such good care of the studio, I promise."

"I know you will," she says. "It's not like there won't be more financial hurdles. This is huge—getting the house. But next year, we'll be looking for a way to pay for college—all four years."

"I'll get a job," I say. "I'll get two! I'll get a scholarship."

Greta looks distracted.

"I will," I say. "You don't believe me?"

"I believe you. I was thinking about something else…I was thinking things looked pretty cozy in there."

"Garbo, relax. We didn't do anything."

"Right," she says.

"I mean we didn't do anything *serious*."

"I'm just saying, from my own experience, sometimes it happens before you're ready for it." She's given me this talk before.

"It won't," I say.

"Just be careful. And when it does happen, whether it's with Sawyer or some other boy, I'm sure I don't have to tell you to use protection."

"No you don't, Garbo, but that's okay. It's endearing that you think I was born yesterday."

On Monday the verdict comes back: Capital murder. On the shows I watch, it's usually called murder in the first degree, but capital murder is apparently what they call it in Texas. It means a murder for which the judge can decide to give the death penalty—capital punishment. But my father gets life in prison without parole, which seems worse, to me.

I once heard a bad joke about a guy who needs to have his leg amputated, due to cancer. He comes out of the operation and says, Doc, how'd it go? and the doctor says, John, I have some good news and some bad news: which would you like first? The patient says, Oh, Doc, give me the bad news first. And the doctor says, We accidentally amputated the wrong leg. No! Doc! Say it ain't so! And the doctor says, But you haven't heard the good news: the other leg turns out to not be cancerous after all!

Ha, ha.

The man gets to keep the one leg, but he never should've

lost any legs. He's supposed to be happy he's not losing both. He's supposed to feel lucky.

I have a generous almost step-father interested in my well-being. But my real father, he's pretty much gone. My mother, she's amputated, too. Good news, bad news. Me, without a leg to stand on. Correction: one prosthetic limb.

CHAPTER THIRTY-THREE

FLESH AND BLOOD

After two weeks of Sawyer being grounded, his parents lift the restriction so it's just school nights that he can't come over. And he is never allowed to stay the night. In their minds, the benefit was our first date; in ours, we'd been waiting for months, and those months counted for something. Sawyer says he knew what he was doing and he doesn't regret it. Mr. and Mrs. Madison know they have a great kid. I intend to prove to them that I am worth his affection.

So we see each other on the weekends. On weeknights, we're both getting more homework done than we would if we were in the same place. I attack mine, finishing in time to watch *48 Hours*.

There's a guy on a killing spree, who ends up killing people in six different states. Many of the bodies are found near tracks. The killer jumps aboard a train after each murder. Gets off the train in another state, just long enough to find someone else to kill. He is partial to couples making out in cars, or on park benches, or (how *convenient!*) at the train tracks. He often uses a sledge hammer. Law enforcement from all six states bands together. Highways in every direction have roadblocks set up—they'll stop every car and look for this man. The one woman who survived his attack helps homicide draw a sketch. They are going to get him and he knows it, so he turns himself in.

Everyone remarks how cold he is, how his eyes are dead—no life or feeling in them at all. Even on TV I see what they're talking about. Eyes like black swamp water. Still as stone.

I feel sorry for him. He's a reflection of all the hatred directed his way.

In Bower's class, we read some stories by Flannery O'Connor. They call her type of stories "Southern Gothic." My favorite is called "A Good Man is Hard to Find," a story about a man known as the Misfit who assassinates an entire family while they're on vacation. O'Connor made parts of it funny, and sort of made the family unlikable first, miserable really, so that you almost cheer when the Misfit guns them all down. Bower challenged us to reread it until we started to get some of the underlying meaning. We talked about it for days in class, until we all had a good enough understanding to write papers on it. I wrote about how the Misfit, in the end, is not only the "good man" of the title, but he's sort of everyman. There's a part right before she's shot when the grandmother says to the Misfit, "Why you're one of my babies. You're one of my own children!" She recognizes him suddenly as *family*. It's like the author is saying the worst man among us is a product of us. He's our own flesh and blood. The Misfit acts out societal ill for us all. Takes it on, almost like Jesus took on all sin.

This man on *48 Hours*, with eyes opaque as motor oil, he's like the Misfit. I'm not saying he's a hero or anything close to Jesus, but he's a product of our messed up world and none of us are blameless.

CHAPTER THIRTY-FOUR

STUDYING THE ODE

Incredibly, life goes on. People go to work, to school. Cars stop at red lights, go at green. Seasons do their thing. Teachers assign homework; I show up for class. I'm a girl with a father who did a horrible thing. I'm a motherless daughter. But there's new dirt for people to gossip about: drunk driving incidents; two of the wait-staff where Kale works caught having sex in the walk-in freezer; and the girl to give the valedictory speech at graduation who will be doing it five months pregnant. The whole McCoy tragedy is so much old news in this town.

In Bower's class, we're reading Pablo Neruda and studying the ode. He wrote odes to so many things: a pair of socks, a kind of chowder, wine, an artichoke, a fish, a lemon, salt. The man could write about a tomato as though he were having sex with it. Doesn't matter if he's writing about a lemon or a chestnut, he will find a way to put in the word *breast* or *nipple*. Or compare the arc of a goblet of wine to the curve of a woman's hip bone.

Bower doesn't even flinch when she reads lines like *Your breast is the grape cluster; your nipples are the grapes*. Or the line,

Oh, to bite into you. Kale and I get into hysterics (and trouble) over these lines. Bower separated us at the beginning of the year, for too much talking and laughing. We are on opposite sides of the classroom, but that doesn't stop us, when Bower reads the word "erect" in "Ode to an Artichoke," from shooting each other a look that unleashes the same hysterics. We don't need proximity. We just need eye contact.

Bower gives us an exercise. Write a list of twenty things you love. You should see how fast the pens move. I'm waiting for her to say, "Okay, now write an ode to one of the things off your list." I'm so sure she's going to say this that I get started on it—"Ode to Cheese." But then she says, "Now, I'd like you to make a list of twenty things you hate." This is equally easy. Everyone's writing frantically when Bower assigns the next part for homework: Write an ode to something off your hate list.

"What?" we say, a chorus of protest and disbelief. Everyone wants to write to their boyfriend or girlfriend or chocolate.

Bower says, "It's easy to write an ode, a tribute, to something you love. It's not as easy, but it's much more interesting, to figure out how to honor something you hate."

Someone says, "Can we make a new hate list, then?"

Bower says no. Pick something off the list you already wrote. Group groan.

Kale walks with me part of the way to my next class.

"Did you like that?" she says. "The artichoke with the erection?"

"I thought the large tuna in the marketplace was pretty darn sexy," I say.

Kale says, "Looks like I'm spending tonight writing an ode to stinky sponges."

"Good one. You should bring in a sample for everyone to

sniff."

We have to head down different hallways before I get to tell her that "Ode to Stinky Sponges" isn't nearly as hard as what I'm going to have to write.

CHAPTER THIRTY-FIVE:

HATE LIST

A couple days later, Bower asks me to stay after class. I try to think if I used swear words in my ode. She's made people change words even in their creative writing, unless the swear word is part of dialogue, and believable as something that would come out of the character's mouth. With an ode, I'm not sure what her rules are.

When the bell rings, I tell Kale to go ahead without me.

"Why?"

"Bower wishes to detain me."

"Detention? What'd you do?"

"No, I'm exaggerating. She said she wants to talk to me."

"May the force be with you."

Bower says not to worry, she'll give me a note for being late to my next class. She pulls a chair up right by her desk. I figure this next period must be one she has off. Maybe it's her lunch period. I've never thought about Bower eating lunch, but I imagine it now: a sandwich, wheat bread, prim, a slim slice of meat inside. Lettuce.

She says, "I'm very impressed by your ode."

I'm not sure what I expected, but it wasn't this.

She goes on. "It is brave; it's original; it's poetic; it's disturbing; it's quite good, I think, especially for your age."

I try to remember exactly what my ode said.

"I'd like your permission to send it to some magazines, see if we can't get it published."

She's made comments all over it, and some suggestions for edits and revisions. I can take her comments home and work on it, and give it back to her before the last day of school. She'll submit it to potential publishers over the summer.

"Thanks," I say. I'm still conjuring it up in my head, thinking there aren't really swear words, though it's definitely adult material. If my ode were a movie, it would be PG, at least.

Bower pulls my paper out of a folder on her desk, where all the odes are stacked. I see Brian Walsh's ode under mine. "Ode to Football." This is intriguing—the ode was to be about something on our hate lists, and Brian Walsh is on the high school football team—varsity. He's been voted Most Valuable Player. Does Walsh secretly hate the game? Do his parents make him play? I find him more interesting, suddenly. I want to read his ode.

"Looks like Brian wrote off of his list of things he loves," I say.

"No," Bower says. "He used his hate list. Yours and his were the best in the class, the most complex. Never assume you know everything about someone. People are complicated."

She hands me my typed poem. There are more words on the page that she wrote than words I wrote. Her suggestions are in purple ink.

"Wow," I say.

"Don't be discouraged," Bower says. "If I write that much on your paper, any paper, it's a very good sign. It means I was engaged, and I care, and I want it to be as good as it can be. But I would never work that hard on your poem if I wasn't already impressed."

As soon as I leave, I go straight to the girls' room, into a stall, to read in private what I wrote, what she wrote. It *is* good, I think. I work on it that night, taking most of Bower's wise suggestions, cutting fat from the poem, sharpening its edges. Deciding what bears repeating.

Ode to a Hoe
by Tate McCoy

Primitive,
prehistoric.
You are an artifact, relic, museum piece.
All those years, all that history
I never knew how
to use you.
The rake, the shovel, straightforward,
their purpose made clear by shape.
What does a hoe do?
You mean a ho or a hoe?
You mean like a rap song, that kinda ho?
I mean weaponry.
What does a hoe do?
Gouge out spade-shaped offerings of dark earth?
(Is that blood on your face?)
Devastate?
(Is that hair?)
She couldn't stay
faithful,
couldn't stay
undrunk,

driven by insatiability.
He couldn't stand it, finally.
When she turned herself toward better,
Like you turned your blade toward her,
When she learned to love a different man
And to build, out of clay,
artifacts
implements
history
vessels.
How dare she?
But you, the hoe of my hate list,
It's not your fault.
Your sawed off handle spot left raw—
What does a hoe do?
You were supposed to help things *grow*.
I miss her,
her hair,
the last ever garden you tended.

CHAPTER THIRTY-SIX:

A THOUSAND BUFFALO

Garbo has a new nickname—Guardian. It's official, from the court. Dad's family fought this, but not with much gusto. They're in a state of shock. The judge talked to me and talked to Greta and talked to Uncle Jim, and then gave me what I wanted. We joke about how Greta has the upper hand she's always wanted, but only till I turn eighteen, which is only three months away. Enjoy it now, I say. Go ahead, lord it over me.

It was Garbo's idea to stop in Santa Fe on our way to Montana. She said 1) it's on the way, so why not?; and 2) it would be good to thank Kevin in person, which it was. Greta and I sent thank-you notes to the address on the check back in January, and when he wrote us back, he repeated that we could visit, any time.

Kevin wants to help with college, too. He has the resources, he said. He told me it was simple. He was in love with my mother; my mother loved me very much. Like if A equals B, and B equals C, then A equals C. He cared about Mom; she cared about me; now he cares about me.

In Montana, we stay in a friend's cabin. Someone Greta

works with has this summer place—she's been before but this is the first time she's taken me. We go to Yellowstone and see about a thousand buffalo. I'm not kidding. You think those animals, the ones on the nickel, don't really exist anymore? Go to Yellowstone and you'll see millions. They're also called bison. There are grizzly bears too, but we haven't seen any. We have bear spray to carry with us on hikes. If you happen to startle a momma bear with cubs, look out—they are fiercely protective of their young.

We're in the middle of Yellowstone, a good two hour's drive from any exit, at a pull-out vista point on the park road, when Greta takes out a cell phone and flips it open to see if she can get reception.

"Lo and behold, is that my aunt with a cellular phone in the wilderness?" I touch her forehead to check for a fever.

She tells me I can shut up now. She's my legal guardian and she can make me.

"I'm so scared," I say.

Greta closes the phone. "A lot of good this would do us if we need it. It just keeps saying 'Searching for Signal.'" We get back in the car.

"When did you even get that?" I ask her.

"A while ago. I rarely use it, and I'm not saying I *like* it."

"Okay," I say.

"But yes, our little incident at the Grand Canyon had an effect on me. I learned something, you could say."

"Garbo learned something from her niece?"

"Garbo did."

I slap my hands together like a seal and do my pleased seal imitation.

"Well," Greta says. "No trip's complete till you've been reduced to zoo noises."

She stops the car for a buffalo in the middle of the road.

It's not the first time. They waltz across the park road as though cars don't even exist. Humans are secondary here, which seems fair.

"Oh give me a home," I sing. "Where the buffalo roam…"

"Where the deer and the antelope play." Greta opens her window and sings to the beast: "Where seldom is heard, a discouraging word."

I finish: "And the skies are not cloudy all day."

"Actually, they are right now," Greta says, looking up. Then she says, "Come on, move it," but the buffalo does not budge.

CHAPTER THIRTY-SEVEN:

MOMMA BEAR

Greta's got the bear spray; I've got the water bottle and camera. Neither of us wears a backpack. We're not planning to go very far. It's our last day at the cabin and we're taking one last hike.

We round a corner and the view opens up: exquisite. Like something you've seen on a postcard. Barns and farms and cows dot the green; cylindrical bales of hay interspersed at exact intervals over the plowed fields. Way down at the bottom of the scene is the Yellowstone River, curving and sparkling its way through a pastoral landscape. Funny, these days I only have to see water—a lake or stream or river—and I can tap into my buoyancy. My mind is trained to it now, a mental state I can reach with just a little thought. I go there now.

We both stop, marveling.

"I want to live right here," Greta says.

We can see forever. To the Beartooths, peaks that still have snow leftover from winter. From here, we see layers and layers of Montana: browns and yellows and greens and hay. All this under a sheet of Montana sky.

I take a few pictures. "Should we call these 'Greta's Future Homestead'? I want to search Montana guys for you, on Cupid.com."

She knows I won't actually do this. Greta broke up with a guy almost three years ago, and I think she's taking the single, independent woman thing a bit too far. She's not likely to do internet romance, seeing how long it has taken her to accept the advent of the cell phone.

We each take a sip from the water bottle, do a perfunctory 360-degree glance to check for bears.

"Honest to God," Garbo says. "Have you ever seen a place so pretty?"

"I'd live here," I say.

"Maybe we should look at colleges for you in Montana or Wyoming!" Garbo gets all ahead of herself. "And I'll live not far away and you can come visit on holidays."

I tease her. "And we'll have a dog and a cat and a horse and a buffalo!"

We start walking again and eventually Greta says, "What is that?" She's heading toward what looks like a site that burned on the top of the hill. There are blackened trees strewn all around, but the fire was so long ago, the grasses have all grown back.

"Oh my God," Greta says. "Come check this out."

If this was a house, all that's left is the foundation—a concrete rectangle, and inside it the charred remains of a family's life. One double bed frame, two singles, a stone hearth, wood-burning stove, metal base of a kitchen table, metal frames of chairs. There's a bathtub; there's a sink. Tall plants and weeds have grown up inside the foundation. Seeds blown in and taken root. A million grasshoppers leap some strange choreography. Something gross, yellow, bubbly (fire retardant?) has hardened all over one edge of the concrete. This place, this burned out home, has the best view of all, the best view in this whole damn valley.

But the more immediate view, the close-up of destruction—I see scorched remnants of shelter, charred reminiscences of a family. I see where the fire came up the mountainside, a wide swath of burned trees. *Had the family been asleep? Was it night or day?* The unexpected nature of it gets to me the most. Never knew it was coming, and then the whole world turns to ash. The metal table where you've had your meals since you were in a high chair, left twisted and contorted by a torrent of searing heat.

Greta gingerly steps through the debris, looking for something to take back to Meg for her sculptures. Grasshoppers bounce all around her. I sit on the edge of the foundation, my feet elevated slightly on the metal remains of a child's box springs. I start to cry.

"Look at this!" Greta says, having discovered a whole set of fireplace implements—a poker, a shovel, the rack that once held the assembled logs aloft. The irony is painful. Of the few things that survive the devastation—the tools the family used to tend the fire, warm the place in winter. Hearth and home and all that. You could write a paper on it for a literature class.

Maybe it's my defeated posture, maybe it's the sight of my sneakers propped on a child's burned bed, maybe my crying is the audible kind, but Greta is there in an instant by my side, nearly killing herself on the way when her foot gets snagged in a snarl of weeds.

I cry for a long time. She holds me. The grasshoppers make their clicking sound.

Funny what your mind goes to and when. I remember some kind of party at my dad's work, a campout. We roasted hot dogs on sticks and for dessert, we roasted marshmallows. The outside of the food turned as black as the remnants of this house. My dad was out of his element and so was my mom, but I was maybe four and didn't know that yet. Didn't know they weren't the type to go camping, or that they weren't happily married. They seemed happy to me. I asked my dad about it much later, when they separated. *What about that time we camped with the other families from your job? Did Mom love us then?* "Tate," he'd said, "she has always loved you, and always will." But in the memory, Mom held me on her lap while I charred marshmallow after marshmallow. I liked the burned, flaky outer part, and the melted, gooey inside. Dad was my assistant, skewering the marshmallows. When I asked him about that night, he said, "Your mother and I fell in love with you the moment we saw you. We might not be good at being married, but we will never stop being your parents and we could never stop loving you, Tate McCoy." He asked me what I wanted more than anything at that moment and I said *Pizza!* We went right then and got one, with extra cheese. I was a nut for cheese, even then.

"My mom and dad weren't really good for each other," I say now. It's the first time I've spoken in a good while.

Greta says, "No, they weren't."

There's some sort of drum among the debris—barrel-shaped, on its side, rusted out.

"What's that?" I point to the end of the burned metal drum thing—the hole at the bottom of it where something sticks out.

Greta sees it. "Is it a tail?"

It disappears, retreats. Then in its place, a tiny beak. Then the head, then the whole wee bird emerges, looks left and right, looks up. We are statue still. She flies to the top of the bed frame, then to the foundation. She darts into the deep brush where we can no longer see her and then emerges with some brambly conglomeration in her beak. She hops back the same way she left, reversing her steps. Edge of foundation, top of bed frame, edge of steel drum, entryway. She disappears inside.

"She's making a nest in there," I say.

"You think it's the male or the female?" Greta says.

"I think it's the momma bird." That sets me off again, and Greta holds me while I let it all out.

"This is all good, Tate," she says.

"Except I'm getting snot on your fleece," I blubber. Then I giggle. I'm in that crazy state where you're crying so pitifully you make yourself laugh.

"Have at it," Greta says. "Consider me a Kleenex, open for business."

We sit there, entwined, long enough to see the little bird make three more foraging trips, always returning with stuff in her beak.

"She's good at building nests," I say. "That stuff she's using is the same plant you got all tangled up in before."

"You're right," Greta says, looking back at the undergrowth. "It just about killed me. Would make a good, tight weave."

I see Greta do the scan of the land around us—the bear scan. Greta, my guardian, my momma bear.

CHAPTER THIRTY-EIGHT:

THAT SCHOOL IN ARIZONA

On the long drive home, Garbo and I talk about colleges. Sawyer and I are thinking about applying to all the same schools. We want to be together, and we like the same colleges anyway.

While Greta approves of Sawyer, she thinks the last thing on my mind right now should be committing to some guy, planning around a relationship.

"I think he might be the love of my life," I say.

Greta almost spews her iced tea.

"What?" I say. "That's mean. He totally could be. You don't know everything."

"It's just that *love of my life* thing. We've been hearing it a lot lately." She switches lanes, and we're quiet for a minute. She says, "You're right, I'm no expert on this stuff. I'm sorry I laughed, I am. But here's what I think."

"Go on," I say. The drive through Colorado is pretty, but

it's taking forever. I'm waiting for the hour to turn, at which point it'll be my turn at the wheel. Driver gets to pick the music. I've had my fill of Garbo's favorite bluegrass CD. And her philosophies on romance. Just because she's single and in her forties, never married, doesn't mean I will go that route.

"From my own experience, guys are going to come and go from your life," she says. "You may not think this now, but *I* think, before you settle down, you are going to have a lot of boyfriends. You *should*. And not just a variety of guys, but a variety of experiences and adventures. You'll travel, you'll graduate college, you'll meet people you can't even imagine right now, you'll find your passion, probably pursue it in graduate school..."

"Have a kid," I interrupt. I'm being ornery. Long car trips make me this way.

"Well, maybe, yes." Garbo is so flexible as to sometimes annoy. She can bend the conversation this way if I insist. "A dozen years or so from now, maybe you'll make a child with some lovely man who deserves to mix his genes with yours."

"Hello," I say. "Are you forgetting my own flawed genetic make-up? Mother: depressed alcoholic. Father: psychopath murderer."

"He's not a psychopath."

"Deranged, then."

"Who knows," she says. "People snap. Even good people. And especially people who always appear to have everything in their lives under tight order and control. They're like a rubber band, stretched past its limit."

"Anyway," I say, "nothing I can do about any of that."

"Precisely. You didn't choose these two parents, nor did you choose such a tragic loss of both of them. But you do get to choose where you go from here, and what you make of your life."

"End of lecture, I hope."

"Almost," she says.

"*What*?" I say. I'm a rubber band past my limit. I'm exasperated. I want to drive. I want quiet. *I miss my boyfriend.*

"When and if the time comes and you make that decision, you will make an outstanding mom."

"Hey," I say, "can I drive?"

We do the switch, high-fiving behind the car, even though it's ten minutes before my turn. She reclines her seat and closes her eyes. The thing is, I know what she says is true. I know deep down there is nothing wrong with me, no inherited insanity. My mom's struggles in life: those are her things, not mine. And my dad's irrational, inexplicable, reprehensible, completely irreversible act? His deal entirely. His to sort out and endure.

All things considered, I feel pretty lucky to have come out of these last two years relatively unscathed.

Tell that to the *Dateline* reporter. *Daughter says she feels lucky.*

1) I've got Sawyer, a perfect boyfriend; 2) I've got a good job; 3) I've got Leafy Green; 4) I've got only one more year of high school; 5) Bower thinks I'm talented; 6) Garbo is a pretty killer guardian, as far as guardians go. And just before we left on this trip, Mags told me about this plan she has. She becomes Maddie's Big, and then she brings her over to the office when I'm working, or sometimes she and Maddie will meet me and Sawyer at Barton Springs. Sawyer's going to teach Maddie to swim. So, 7) I get Maddie back.

Then there's my father, who I may stay mad at forever. I have no desire to see him. But my thoughts turn to him sometimes, in a sympathetic way. As good and full as my life feels right now, I bet his feels proportionately terrible. You can feel sympathy for a person you despise. You can miss the person he used to be. He's ruined every conceivable thing. He's *Doing Life*. Funny how they call it that, when it is just about as far from actual living as one could get.

Garbo is asleep, deep into one of her power naps. I should be nicer to her. She's great. I think about Sawyer, how many days it's been since we've kissed. Two weeks. *Too many*. I think I want to go see that school in Arizona. I like the plants there—the cacti—how they store up water inside themselves and can go such a long time without rain. I can conjure up a scene from the edge of the Grand Canyon easily. All above you and below you are rocks—different layers, that tell the history of the canyon being carved out by the river. The rocks have big cracks in them, and you'll see a cactus just jutting out horizontally, asserting itself straight out of the sheer cliffs, hanging. Everything would indicate these cacti should hurtle to their deaths—a shallow root system, a *crack* for a home, so little soil in which to plant themselves—the mere fact of the plants' weight and position and gravity working against them every day.

But they hold tight; they hang on.

They survive.

They thrive.

About Melanie Bishop

Melanie Bishop writes fiction, nonfiction and screenplays, and has taught all of these subjects for the past twenty-one years as a professor at Prescott College in Arizona. Her memoir, *Some Glad Morning*, will be published in 2014 by Outpost 19. Her short stories have appeared in numerous literary magazines, including *Glimmer Train, Greensboro Review,* and *Georgetown Review*. Melanie is founding editor and fiction and nonfiction editor of *Alligator Juniper*, Prescott College's award-winning national literary magazine. *My So-Called Ruined Life* is her first Young Adult novel. Find Melanie online at **melaniebishopwriter.wordpress.com**.

Acknowledgements

I would like to thank all of the following: Mrs. Bauer, my 11th grade English teacher at O.Perry Walker, for getting me started in this whole writing thing; She Writes and Girls Write Now for their early encouragement on this novel, when they named it a winner in their YA contest; Lisa Marcusson for her support, encouragement, expertise, and friendship throughout the writing and marketing process; good friend and fellow writer Ellen Winter for suggesting Torrey House Press; Mark, Kirsten, and Anne at Torrey House for bringing the book to print and challenging me to make it better; Hannah Rose Smith, Allie Field Bell, and Eliot Treichel for being early readers who gave me crucial feedback; SCBWI, Nevada chapter, for the Tahoe conference; Beth Bauman, Martha Baden, Kathleen Jeffrie Johnson, Susan Lang, and Christy Seifert for writing blurbs; Lynn Walterick for research and feedback on query letter; the staff at Wild Basin in Austin, for providing necessary info; Deb Ford for her friendship and her Upper Hawk Valley house, where I wrote the bulk of the first draft; Katy Edelson for her family's cabin in the redwood forest, where I wrote the bulk of the final draft; Playa at Summer Lake for the generous residency and the inspiration; indispensable best writer friends Laura Didyk and Bob Schirmer; all my students and colleagues, past and present, at Prescott College; Mary Odem for her forever friendship and for brainstorming plot details by phone; Leah Gilbert Odem and Sam Coodley for the great promotional video; Christy Hawkins for the lovely cover art; and Ted Bouras for every single thing, for being perfect.

Thanks also to all the wild places.

About Torrey House Press

The economy is a wholly owned subsidiary of the environment,
not the other way around.
—Senator Gaylord Nelson, founder of Earth Day

Love of the land inspires Torrey House Press and the books we publish. From literature and the environment and Western Lit to topical nonfiction about land-related issues and ideas, we strive to increase appreciation for the cultural importance of natural landscape through the power of pen and story. Through the 2% to the West program, Torrey House Press donates two percent of sales to not-for-profit environmental organizations and funds a scholarship for up-and-coming writers at colleges throughout the West.

Visit **www.torreyhouse.com** for discussion guides, author interviews, and more.